THE CONFEDERATE FIDDLE

J. R. WILLIAMS

THE
CONFEDERATE
FIDDLE

Prentice-Hall, Inc. · Englewood Cliffs, N. J.

For Patricia,
Friend of my heart,
Whose great-grandfather, Benjamin Redford,
fought with Rip Ford
in the last battle of the Civil War.

CONTENTS

RED RIVER

After a dry winter, spring, and summer, this first day of September in 1863 didn't promise anything but eating more dust. The nine wagons in front of Vin Clayburn were churning up plenty. Calloused hands firm on the lines, Vin ran his tongue over his lips, made a disgusted face. The inside of his mouth was as dry as the outside. It seemed more like five thousand miles they'd traveled than the actual five hundred; more like years than forty days since they'd left home in Missouri. And they were still a mighty long way from Brownsville on the Mexican border, a long way from the last open port of the Confederacy.

Beside Vin, Roncador played his bullwhip between his fingers and squinted at the lowering sun. The grizzled old buffalo hunter was Vin's swamper or assistant. He cooked for the train, too, as the man least likely to ruin the food.

"We'll hit the Red River before dark," he roared above the sound of the wagons. "You may get your feet washed."

"You can't scare me," Vin retorted. "Some water'll look good."

"Yep. And the Red makes it about halfway to Brownsville." Roncador poked Vin in the ribs with the whip handle. " 'Course the going really gets tough in Texas. Wind, dry camps, sand—"

"You're the encouraging sort," said Vin.

He looked back at his load, stowed in the blue body of the

prairie schooner. Twelve bales. That was six thousand pounds of fine cotton picked from the Clayburn fields, and two other wagons also carried the family's bales. Mark Morrisey, who drove in the lead, owned two wagons and had the responsibility of five more that belonged to neighbors.

Vin chuckled as Mark's booming voice wafted dimly back. Talking to the mules, the big redhead was. So strong through his broad shoulders and arms that a person would wonder why he wasn't off fighting till they saw his maimed leg, Mark could play a fiddle till it cried or laughed, and the people with it. He could sing *Barbara Allen* so the sweet sadness melted your bones, or wicked, lilting songs of the river. Back home, no one had a party without making sure Mark would be there, and Darcy, too. Darcy, Vin's older brother, was almost as good with the fiddle as Mark. He was riding scout for the train.

Sure hadn't wanted to make this trip, Darcy. He wanted to go off and soldier. No more than I do, though! Vin thought, with a rush of fierce disgust for the reins he was holding. He squeezed them hard, thinking about the cotton that had him trapped on this stifling road south.

It had been planted a year ago last April when Farragut took New Orleans and closed the South's greatest port. Cotton had felt the choke of the Union blockade before but with New Orleans in Yankee hands, things got desperate.

How was the South's one great money crop to be sold to the hungry mills of France, Germany, and England? How could the Confederacy get the arms, munitions and drugs that had to come from Europe? With Union warships patrolling the South's coastline, there was only one port left to the South, one place where cotton could be sold to foreign merchants in return for hard money or supplies.

Through Brownsville, at the southeastern tip of Texas, and her sister Mexican city, Matamoros, just across the Rio Grande, flowed cotton from nearly all growers west of the Mississippi.

At this "backdoor of the Confederacy," cotton that would sell in Missouri or Arkansas or north Texas for ten cents a pound brought as much as seventy and eighty cents—in gold, not the depreciated Confederate paper money.

Besides the profit made by the government on bales handled by its agents, the Confederacy got a tenth of the profit from private cotton like that on Vin's wagon and the other wagons in this train. The remote international port on the Rio Grande was the South's frail lifeline, its last resource in a war with an industrialized North that manufactured for itself what the South had to import.

The cotton crop now baled up in Vin's wagon had matured and picking had begun in late August, when brighter news came for the South. At Second Manassas, where Mark Morrisey had almost lost his leg, the Confederacy gave the Union a crushing defeat. But that was a year ago. Since then had come the fall of Vicksburg, and Gettysburg's bitter losses in early July. The Clayburns were packing the last of these bales into the wagons when Mark brought that news. They had stopped and stared at each other, Darcy, Pa, and Vin.

"Pa, I got to go fight!" Darcy had burst out. "I'm almost eighteen. Drivin' cotton's all right for Vin but—"

"The money this cotton will bring the government can help just as much as soldiers," said James Clayburn in his slow, calm way. "War's not what you think. I had plenty of it in the war with Mexico seventeen years ago."

"So, am I just supposed to sit on my hands while everyone else fights?" Darcy steamed. He had their mother's dark French looks, her grace of motion—her temper, too. "Cousin Tom killed, Cousin Slade wounded, and little Harry gone when he's a year younger than me?"

Their Kentucky cousins. When they visited the Missouri Clayburns several years ago, Vin had envied their rapier-quick style which Darcy shared, along with their recklessness and high good spirits. Vin knew himself to be like Pa. Big-boned, lanky, hair discouraged between tow and buff, long jaw and winter blue eyes. Plain Scotch-Irish. It was good stock, and a solid build—but oh, to be like Darcy!

"You'll deliver this cotton," Pa had said, as they stood by the wagons with Gettysburg's bad news heavy on them. He looked at Darcy till rebellious dark eyes fell before stern blue ones. "When you're conscripted, you'll have to serve, but I won't let you volunteer."

"But—"

Pa watched Darcy. The young man ground white teeth into his lip and went back to loading. "I'll see the cotton to Texas," he said. "But after that—"

He hadn't finished and no one asked him what he meant. After a few days on the long drive, though, he had become his usual rollicking self, and began playing his fiddle after they made camp. He'd even taught Jare Wheelwright, the wrangler, how to play, which made Vin a little jealous. Vin had no gift for music, though he loved to hear it. But Jare was such a funny person. Of course, he was a Quaker. What else could you expect? Vin sniffed. Let an enemy walk all over you? Turn the other cheek?

No, sir! Just as soon as he got old enough, he was going to get in the war—join Darcy, who'd surely be there first in spite of Pa. Vin squinted.

There came Darcy now, wheeling to ride alongside Mark.

Telling the wagon leader what lay ahead, probably. After a minute, Darcy brought his gray loping back to Vin. The horse was wet. Red mud plastered its fetlocks. Darcy's trousers clung wetly to his thighs and water sloshed out of his high boots, but his grin split his dark narrow face as if he'd just found treasure.

"Red River, little brother! Let's dye these old mules! Hey, Roncador, doesn't that Texas breeze tickle your nose?"

"Texas dust!" humphed Roncador. "You'll get a-plenty of it the next few months."

"Now, I sort of doubt that," Darcy laughed.

He rode on ahead to lead across the ford. Mark's yelling really got loud now, and as each wagon in turn went down the bank and lurched across the baked mud flats to the sluggish, clay-stained river, the drivers used whips, threats, and prayers to urge their reluctant teams into the water.

"Gee up!" Vin whooped, playing out the twelve-foot lash so the buckskin popper cracked ferociously without hitting anything. "Gee up, you long-eared Republicans!"

"Don't insult honest mules," said Roncador.

Luckily, this was a gradual ford. The wagon came down into the water with comparatively little splash and wrench. But such a heavy load made any crossing hard. The wheels turned with maddening chugs, gurgling in the thick water that churned up to the floorboards. The near wheel mule lost its footing, started slipping sideways, pulling its mates out of line, swaying the wagon. Darcy rode in, buoying the animal back on its feet, helping Vin get the team back in the shallows.

Roncador looked at Vin. "Whew!"

"Thanks, Darcy!" Vin called. Darcy flourished his soft gray hat.

"A pleasure," he bowed. "Always glad to help those who need it—women, kid brothers—" His grin took the bite from the words as he swung his horse ahead of the column but Vin felt himself coloring hotly.

He longed to be like Darcy, but was just born different, apt to bungle when Darcy knew exactly what to do and how. What hurt was for Darcy, so blithely, to take Vin's shortcomings for granted.

As the team strained across the sand bar and scrub willows, Roncador said, "Somebody has to be the youngest, lad. And when Darcy's one hundred, you'll be a spry ninety-eight."

"Huh!" grunted Vin. "Darcy's going to be a doctor! He'll know how to keep healthy while I go to seed."

Roncador laughed, shaking his head. "Doesn't work that way. A doctor knows what to tell other folks but he's too busy with them to take care of himself." He wheezed out his cheeks. "Well, now we're in Texas. We run into any natives, Vin, you remember they figger they're a different breed of cat than us and that they're doin' the Confederacy a favor to join up. Texas was a republic for almost ten years and it's never got over it."

"Weren't you down here during the Mexican War?"

"Clear to the Rio Grande. Then through Mexico till we took the capital in the fall of '47. Never thought I'd be coming back."

Vin looked curiously at Roncador. In his late fifties, the graying teamster had driven trade wagons from Missouri to Santa Fe when that commerce was flourishing, and had been a friend of Kit Carson. Driving everything from Chihuahua carts to Conestogas, Roncador had whacked mules, oxen, horses, and probably people, to judge from the scars on his face. One stretched across a permanently flattened nose which nightly emitted the thunderous snores that gave him his nickname. Roncador meant "The Snorer." The Santa Fe Mexicans had given him the title, and he wore it as he did the bullwhip marks, with swagger. No one knew his real name, and he seemed to have forgotten it.

As the wagon train rolled along the Texas bank of the river, the sun dyed everything with a final glow of red-gold. Mark Morrisey's bellow floated back.

"Cor—ral!"

Five of the wagons swung left. The last five, including Vin's, circled right to curve till they met the end of the other string, while Mark's wagon halted behind Vin's.

They now had an oval corral with openings at both ends. Unhitching the mules, the teamsters drove them to the river and let them drink. Darcy helped Vin because Roncador, as cook, had started right in at that job. As they brought the mules back from the water, running them inside the corral to graze, Vin looked with pleasure at the sere but plentiful grass.

"Won't have to feed grain tonight."

Darcy nodded. He seemed to have his mind on something else, though he took care to fasten the rope that closed the gap at their end of the oval. Faintly troubled, Vin stretched and spoke loudly.

"That old river's not much to look at, but at least it's wet."

"And we're in Texas." Darcy had been staring to the northeast. He turned now, suddenly. "I'm leaving the train, Vin. Now—tonight."

"Why—what—?" Vin almost tripped over a wagon tongue. "What you talking about, Darcy?"

In the dim light Vin saw with a sinking heart that his brother's jaw was set in the steel-spring way that meant he was determined to do a thing. He said, "I'm going to the war. I'll get in the cavalry if I can, but wherever they put me, I'm through watching."

Vin felt first numb inside, then sick, as if he'd been kicked in the stomach. Darcy take off like this, do what Vin wanted to more than anything on earth? "You can't!" Vin blurted. "You promised Pa—"

"That I'd see this cotton to Texas. Haven't I?"

A trembling began in Vin, working outwards till he had to clench his hands to keep them from shaking. He wanted to yell or, in Roncador's language, bawl like a baby. This way Darcy had of getting around rules was a thing Vin tried not to think of. But when it hit him in the face like this, he had to. The last time, it'd been over a dance Pa had told Darcy not to attend. Darcy promised not to ride there, but he had *walked*—and then been so contritely surprised over the "mis-understanding" that Pa let him off with a blessing-out. When Vin disobeyed, he did it outright and got thrashed just as straightforwardly.

Usually Vin envied, rather than condemned, Darcy's merry-hearted evasions—but this wasn't any dance! He squared his shoulders.

"That's not what Pa thought you meant, and you know it!"

Darcy's mouth clamped down, pulling brown skin tight over well-made cheekbones. "I can't help what he thought, Vin. Our cousins are dead or fighting. All the men my age are gone but the cowards!" He broke off, swallowing. When he spoke again, it was with his old, bantering smile. "Don't preach, little brother. You want to go almost as bad. Aren't you going to wish me luck?"

Trying to harden himself against the coaxing voice, Vin stared at his dusty, mud-covered boots. Darcy had been plan-ning this all the time and hadn't breathed a word, though now

Vin would have the full responsibility for the cotton. But even in Vin's angry hurt, Darcy's presence reached in and made Vin see things from his brother's standpoint, understand that being thought a conscript-dodger was unbearable to Darcy.

"I guess I'd have to wish you luck whatever you did, Darcy. But Pa's going to feel like you lied to him—and you *did,* whatever the words you used." Vin wanted to add, *You're not doing me right, either;* but he couldn't, not to Darcy, who was mostly just what Vin wanted desperately to be.

Darcy's shrug was uncomfortable. "Blazes, Vin! I can't mess around on a job that's been taken over by kids, cripples, cowards and old men!" Vin winced. Punching him in the ribs, Darcy said quickly, "Well, you are a kid, but it's nothing you won't grow out of. Come on, let's eat."

Vin felt as if each step he took plunged him through a trapdoor but he tried to make his stride as nonchalant as Darcy's. No one else was going to know how he felt about this. Outside the wagons, Roncador was rustling up sowbelly and beans, coffee, and sour dough biscuits, while he growled at Mark Morrisey.

"Eat it and grin like it's good or cook your own!"

Mark winked at the others, green eyes dancing. A person hardly noticed his staved-in knee that gave a list to his walk. *My little souvenir of Second Manassas,* he'd say, and add proudly, *We almost ran those Yankees into the Potomac!* Even with his smashed knee, no one cared to heckle Mark. He had to vent most of his bursting strength on his blacksmith's anvil which he ran in addition to his delta land farm. A good man, Mark, for work or jokes or fighting.

"In the army we had meat built into our bread—weevils. Now there was cooking for you, Roncky!" Mark's voice caressed the cook, whose big ears were turning a brilliant red. "I've eaten everything from roots to snakes but durn if I ever tasted anything like what you do with sowbelly and beans."

"And I've cooked over everything from driftwood to mountain goat chips," Roncador shot back, "but I never smelled anything like you! Move out of the drift of the wind, Mark Morrisey, so's I can tend to my cooking without gettin' sick!"

Mark lounged off, chuckling, and settled himself against a wagon wheel with his pipe. The other men were sprawled around by now, tired, sweaty, but in good spirits from having crossed the river, almost the half-way mark of their journey. What Darcy had said was true. Though teamstering was hard work, the war had taken those who used to do it. Of the twenty-two men with the train, only Darcy and Trig Medders were of combat age and condition. Trig, twenty, hulking, but strong as a horse, was scared of plain fist fights unless he caught a boy much smaller than himself. He kept out of Darcy's way, for Darcy had said loudly several times what he thought of men who evaded the conscription by taking work as cotton haulers. The government figured the trains were so important that teamsters could be excused from military service. Vin glanced hastily away from Trig.

Blending his pipe's smoke with Mark Morrisey's was Tim Sullivan, known as Sully. A tinker before leaving Ireland in his youth, he lived alone in a shanty on the river, doing odd jobs and helping at harvest. Mama said he reminded her of a leprechaun, with his bowed, thin legs and aureole of white hair. Still, there was an amazing toughness in his bent form and he handled his wagon as handily as any man. He hopped up nimble as a rabbit when Roncador banged on a skillet, signaling the food was ready.

Filling their tin plates and cups, the men sat or squatted to wolf their food. Jare Wheelwright, the wrangler, stopped by Vin and Darcy, seemed almost ready to sit down, but when Vin watched his plate instead of speaking, the thin dark boy moved on.

"What you got against him?" Darcy asked, frowning.

"Nothing," Vin said tightly.

Jare couldn't help it—maybe—if he was a Quaker, but Vin plain couldn't understand him. No spunk, always reading, teacher's pet. Their last year in school, Jare had been sent after drinking water and Vin had sneaked a mud puppy into the bucket. One of the girls had gone for a drink and near yelled her head off. The teacher whacked Jare good. Jare, though he must have had a good notion that Vin, who sat next the bucket, was guilty, hadn't said a word.

Vin had appeased his conscience by thinking, *Old Jare's just scared I'd whale him harder'n the teacher did if he told.* In his heart Vin knew better, though, and had felt mean and little for days. Doggone a boy anyway who didn't act like a boy!

Vengefully spearing a hunk of fat meat, Vin scowled and chewed. "Have you told Mark you're going?" he asked Darcy.

"Not yet."

"Sure wish you'd wait till we get back from the Rio," Vin muttered, jabbing at the slippery beans.

"Well, I'm not going to, Vin, so forget it. Now we're past most of the rivers a scout won't be needed too often and when one is, a swamper can climb off the wagon and ride ahead."

Mark strolled over, folded himself down beside them. "Get your fiddle, Darcy. Let's have a tune." In answer to a reproving glance from Elkanah Crawford, a Primitive Baptist preacher who hoped to get his church a fine bell from his pay for this drive, Mark grinned. " 'Make a joyful noise', Brother Elkanah—that's scripture."

Darcy got his fiddle from its careful wrappings under the wagon seat. Someday he'd own the Stradivarius, passed down from mother's family along with the French heirloom furniture. But this fiddle played sweet. Mark took his mouth organ. Then, as they had done so often, they played little skirls and flirted tunes at each other till they struck "Sourwood Mountain."

It rose, shivered through tired bones, set blood humming. Soon they were all singing except Brother Elkanah, and even he tapped his foot and looked as if he were following the notes deep in his throat. Jare came to lean behind Darcy but Vin somehow didn't grudge it now. Here in Texas, they seemed closer, more of a piece and place, than they had back home. This night singing, with the dark around their fire ringing them together by the wagons, took the edge off their weariness, soothed tempers made jagged by the day's aggravations.

> I don't want none of your weevily wheat
> And I don't want none of your barley.
> All I'll take is your finest flour
> To bake a cake for Charlie—

After awhile, Darcy stood up. He set the fiddle to his chin, courted it like a lover so that everyone hushed to listen to him.

> I know where I'm going and I know who's going with me.
> I know who I love but my dear knows who I'll marry—

And later, with a kind of finality to it that prickled Vin's flesh, Darcy ended with the plaintive turtledove song.

See how that she doth mourn for her true love
As I, my love, shall mourn for thee,
As I shall mourn for thee—
Ten thousand miles seems very far away
For you to return to me—

When he had finished, he straightened. In the fire-shadows he looked tall and grim—a stranger. Vin's heart caught and jerked as he thought, *What if he doesn't come again? What if something happens?*

"It was good singing. I'll remember it." Darcy looked at Mark. "I guess it's time to tell you. I'm going to join the army."

Mark's great shoulders rose, settled as if he forced them. His green eyes searched Darcy's. "Be you? Spite of how your Pa feels?"

"He can't expect me to stay out forever like I was crippled or a kid," blurted Darcy. He reddened, gaze dropping to Mark's bent knee. "I—I mean—"

Mark shrugged but he was pale around the mouth. "I'm not ashamed of my leg. I fought while I could and now I'll get this cotton through. I know how you feel, Darcy, but think twice before you go against your father and toss up the work you began."

Bright spots burned in Darcy's cheeks. "I'm sorry, Mark. I just can't stay out of it any longer!" In the awkward silence, he handed his fiddle to Jare. "You take care of this. Play it nights."

"I can't keep your fiddle!" Jare protested, but his face lighted with pleasure. Darcy thrust it into his hands.

"I'd get it broke fighting and riding. You can give it back to me after the war."

Turning, Darcy moved away. Vin followed. He wanted to

say, *I'm your brother! Why'd you leave your fiddle with Jare instead of me?* Vin couldn't play it, of course, but he was still hurt. He caught Darcy's gray, saddled it, helped his brother fasten on his bedroll and saddlebags. Settling his rifle into the scabbard, Darcy hesitated a second before he caught Vin's shoulder, gave it a roughly affectionate shake.

"So long, kid."

Vin couldn't speak. As the gray moved off, Vin followed in the dark, to the river, heard the splashing that meant Darcy was on his way back out of Texas—on his way to where things were happening. Vin squeezed his hands tight.

If he could go, too! Share the danger and glory. But, no, he had to wallop mules along with conscript dodgers like Trig and pious fellows like Jare. How come Darcy, who loved a fight more than anyone, had any use for that Quaker?

All sound from the river had stopped long before Vin made his way back to camp. The hair at the back of his neck prickled as he saw Jare cuddling the fiddle beside the dying fire, caressing the strings with the bow. Jare didn't envy Darcy, that was plain, didn't regret his leaving, either, since it left him with the fiddle.

Crawling into his blankets, Vin listened till his stomach had twisted into a tight knot of jealousy and grief. Darcy, after dumping the family cotton on him, had gone off to the war, and had entrusted his precious fiddle to sober-sided, psalm-singing Jare instead of his own brother!

Why don't I go, too? Vin thought as a fierce stab of temptation pierced him. *Just sneak off tonight? Mark would sell the cotton—it'd be managed someway.*

Oh, sure, he quarreled back at himself. *Roncador could do two men's work on top of cooking and even if it did work out finally and Pa got the money, do you want to make the family beholden to Mark and the others for doing what you and Darcy should have?* Blinking at the hot sting in his eyes, Vin knew he couldn't duck out, especially since Darcy had. What made it even worse was that to outsiders Darcy would be a hero while he, Vin, would seem a slacker. The crooning fiddle sawed at Vin's nerves. On and on. Jerking up, he tossed off the covers, glared at Jare.

"Say—you aim to keep that up all night?"

The fiddle gave a last startled trill. Jare rose, a painfully thin shadow against the embers' glow. "Sorry, Vin." Holding the fiddle with great care, he faded into the scatter of sleeping men.

Mad at everyone, disgusted and ashamed of himself, Vin huddled the covers around his ears, gritted his teeth as Roncador's snores began their rhythmic increase. Was this the way it was going to be the rest of the trip?

WARDELL BEAUREGARD JIMS

The last thing Vin heard was Roncador's snoring and the first sound he heard on waking next morning was Roncador's banging on a skillet.

"Rise and shine!" yelled the cook. In response to hoots and groans, he banged louder. "Come on, you lazy critters! I been up an hour while you sawed logs!"

"Fair enough," rumbled Mark, rolling over and coming to his feet. "You keep everyone awake till we faint off from sheer exhaustion. Know what you sound like?"

Roncador's voice took on a silken purr. "The voice of sweet angels, Mr. Morrisey—if ye're wanting your breakfast."

Ducking under Roncador's arm, Mark filled his plate with biscuits, pork and gravy, and beans left from last night. At a safe distance he turned and grinned.

"You sound like a storm roarin' through the Shenandoah Valley," he said. "Or maybe more like the mortars at Manassas." While Roncador's broad cheeks puffed out, Mark frowned, struck the side of his head in sudden remembrance. "No, by grannies, I finally got it! I was in a mine once when it caved. Last night I woke up and fair hollered, thinkin' the shafts were caving in on me. Then I remembered it was just you."

Roncador's eyes snapped but a chuckle escaped him as he said ferociously, "Hope you get the biscuit I stuck a rock in."

"Wouldn't taste any different from the one I've got."

By now everyone was eating, downing the bitter "coffee." Vin wasn't sure which of the substitutes this was. Tasted like a mixture of rye and corn. The South had used about everything from roasted acorns to sweet potatoes in place of coffee but it all tasted pretty sorry.

"How'd you get this wonderful brew?" Mark was joshing. "Boil a mule shoe in some mud?"

Busy eating, Roncador ignored this thrust, but the men laughed. Vin, too. As he crunched the sour dough biscuits and sopped them in gravy, he thought how lucky the train was to have Mark. His jokes made fun of their troubles. A train that started the day in good spirits was much better able to handle whatever happened. Darcy's fiddle had helped that way too—almost like medicine.

A lump rose in Vin's throat. Darcy was gone. And Jare had his fiddle.

Cleaning his plate from habit though he was all of a sudden no longer hungry, Vin dumped his tin plate and utensils in the bucket of soapy water Roncador had heating and set about harnessing and watering the team. By the time the wagons were ready to move, Roncador had the cook stuff stored away in their wagon, and the sun was starting to edge up. Vin climbed into the wagon, settled by the cook, and wondered if everybody else was as sick of his seat—and job—as he was of his.

"Gee there!" Mark cracked his whip, beginning another day's drive. "Gee up there, you overgrown jack rabbits!"

Amid wild snapping of whips and wilder language, the big blue and red wagons, one by one, rolled southwest, groaning and squeaking as if they were as reluctant as their drivers. As the last wagoners, Vin and Roncador were soon eating dust. But yesterday Darcy had been around, riding back often to tease—but also, Vin knew, to make sure his brother was all right. Vin didn't know he'd let out a long breath till Roncador spoke.

"What's the matter, kid?"

Vin only gave part of his thought. "Texas sure is a big place."

"That it is," Roncador nodded emphatically. "And us on the far end from where we're going."

"Wonder what it'll be like down there."

"Like nothing you've ever seen." Roncador squinted back through the years. "I remember we built Fort Texas—it's Fort Brown now, after Major Brown who was killed there— while right across the river Mexican soldiers raised earthworks to protect their mortars and guns. We looked down each others' throats till it all came to a head at Palo Alto and Resaca de la Palma—it was an awful slaughter of Mexicans. At Resaca de la Palma they had almost two thousand men killed or wounded to our thirty-three dead and eighty-nine wounded. Old Rough and Ready knew what he was doing."

"Didn't the Mexicans fight?"

"Sure they did. But their officers mostly didn't look after them, marched 'em thirty, even fifty miles a day. And even close up they couldn't hit us. My lieutenant checked their cartridges and found out why. Their cartridges held twice as much powder as needed. And maybe you think that doesn't give an awful kick and recoil!"

Vin shivered. That didn't sound like a very glorious kind of war. "There's some kind of war in Mexico now, isn't there?"

"Yep. The French are trying to put an Austrian bigwig over Mexico, an emperor they call him. The Mexicans have their own president, Juárez, so they're fighting tooth and nail to drive the foreigners out."

Vin stared. "What call did France have to mix in the government?"

"It's too complicated for me," said Roncador, scratching his head. "Boiled down, Mexico's been in so many wars that she's had no time to build up the country or get prosperous. The government was in debt to France, England, and Spain when Juárez finally took over from that rascal Santa Ana. Juárez couldn't and wouldn't pay so the European countries decided to come over and collect. England and Spain gave up the idea and called their troops home. But France is trying to cram this Maximilian down the Mexicans' throats so he can get her money back for her."

"Well, if that's so and they have a war going on, how can we send cotton through Mexico?"

Roncador's laugh was a harsh bark. "Ah, lad, war's when some men in any country get rich and the merchants of Matamoros have a long reputation for coming out ahead no matter who's in power."

"Matamoros?" Vin struggled with the unfamiliar name.

"The place across from Brownsville where our cotton goes. We can't ship from Point Isabel anymore because the Yankees are sitting out in the Gulf with their men-of-war. Now, the cotton goes into Matamoros, is put under the name of a Mexican owner, and carried out to the big foreign vessels by little steamboats that are, at least on paper, owned by Mexicans."

Whistling in wonderment, Vin asked, "Don't the Yanks know what's going on?"

" 'Course, but what can they do? They search the Mexican ships and demand proof of neutral ownership of the bales—which they get, signed all legal and binding by high Mexican officials. The Yanks know dang well the cotton is from the Confederacy and that the Confederacy will get the money from it, or the war supplies the foreign ships bring. Still, the Yanks can't seize the cotton without starting a war with Mexico. And that's how it works."

Trig Medders, who had turned his wagon over to his swamper while he rode on to scout for a nooning spot, came riding back. In spite of exposure to sun, he managed to stay a grubby pink and his lank brown hair was almost black with grease where it stuck out from under his hat. He looked at Vin with a twist to his pale, wide mouth.

"Wonder how old Darcy's making out on his lonesome? Don't see how he'll anyways survive without that fiddle."

The back of Vin's neck prickled like the hackles of an angry hound. "He'll need his rifle where he's going. Find a camp site?"

Trig's eyes flared, the yellow shade of a chicken hawk's, but he decided not to push. "There's water about an hour ahead," he answered sullenly, and fell back to the herd of spare animals Jare tended.

Vin scowled. Trig would take his spite out on Jare, who, poor-spirited thing he was, wouldn't know how to tell him off. Well, Vin wished Darcy hadn't gone off against Pa's will and he was jealous about the fiddle. But no one else was going to know it, and they better watch what they said.

It lacked maybe an hour of noon when they reached the small creek and swung into corral. After the stock was watered, the men closed the corral ropes and scattered out to rest. They'd be here three or four hours. Even on good grass, it took a mule an hour to fill up. When the graze was fair, as it was here, it paid to give the animals plenty of time to take advantage of it and they needed the rest anyway on this long a drive. The wagons carried some grain but this was to be used only when the stock had to have it.

Vin wandered over to where Roncador was roasting some kind of meal to use for coffee. In the hottest sun sat the sour dough keg, put there during stops to keep the contents fermenting. The same "start" of soured dough had kept them in bread and biscuits the whole trip. For each baking Roncador took out just enough dough to raise his bread. Then he dumped more flour, salt, and water in the keg to keep the sour dough going. The bread he baked in his treasured Dutch oven, a covered, black, cast-iron pot.

"Sowbelly again?" Vin asked. Needlessly, because they hadn't brought any other meat. Once in a while they bought a stringy beef or shot game, but mostly they had the salty pork. Roncador gave his odorous grindings a stir, coughed, and backed away. He surveyed Vin through streaming eyes.

"Go shoot a squirrel if you crave a change. If you boys did more hunting on these noon stops, we'd eat better."

"Fair enough," Vin said. "Going to need something to take away the taste of that coffee. What is it this time, powdered stink-weed?"

Dodging a pebble Roncador threw after him, Vin got his Sharps rifle and took off on foot. Jare Wheelwright looked up from Darcy's fiddle as if he'd like to come, too, but Vin avoided the silent question. He'd hunt and Jare could fiddle.

When he came back an hour later, Vin put two squirrels and a rabbit down by Roncador.

"Right through the eye, all of 'em!" Roncador exclaimed. "You that good or just lucky?"

"Pa taught us to shoot that way," Vin said casually, but he flushed with pleasure.

"Well, I see why they call a good shot a 'Clayburn' back home," nodded Roncador. Vin's triumph faded. *A Clayburn.*

Of course. His marksmanship was the result of Pa's teaching.
Darcy was just as good, and considerably faster.

Vin set to cleaning the game, handed it on to Roncador
who dredged it in flour and stuck it to simmer over the fire.
Vin had time to catch a short rest in the shade of the wagon
before Roncador gave the dinner signal.

Roncador had made a big kettle of thick gravy to surround
small morsels of meat. It went mighty well with the biscuits
and even put a kind of forgiveness on the inevitable beans
and counterfeit coffee.

Vin, and most of the others, were working on their helpings
when two men rode into the clearing. The one leading had a
hound-dog face and moustachios, was string-bean scrawny.
The other, astride a little mule, was short and plump as if
he'd been eating the provender of his friend as well as his own.
As he rode, legs swinging against the bowed-down mule, he
smacked lustily over some kind of bone. For a moment Vin
thought he knew them. Then he remembered.

Why, they were out of the frontispiece of his book of *Don
Quixote!* Fat Sancho and skinny knight. And the leader's
clothing could scarcely have been more outlandish had it been
that of Spanish knightdom.

His greasy, slouched, gray hat was caught up on one side
by a plume and medallion. Black frock coat, ruffly shirt bosom,
and string tie mixed oddly with buckskin leggings and high-
heeled boots. Sancho's butternuts were singular only for being
so grimy that they had a slick sheen. The skinny man pulled
in his mount, a hapless gray beast with jutting hipbones who
stole the chance to crop a few mouthfuls of grass while his
master doffed his hat and showed teeth as long and yellow as
his charger's.

"Good afternoon, gentlemen. May I address the er-ah—head of this train?"

Mark didn't rush to get to his feet and didn't offer his hand at all. "I'm in charge, mister. My name's Morrisey. You got business with us?"

"Not in my own humble person as Wardell Beauregard Jims, Colonel, Retired, CSA—retired for reasons of health, suh." Those teeth again in a cavernous smile. "But as a representative of the Texas State Military Board and the Cotton Bureau, I welcome you to our beautiful, lately sovereign state."

"Thanks," said Mark.

Wardell Beauregard Jims, Colonel, Retired, chose to flow on in spite of the short reply. "As you are no doubt aware, Captain Morrisey, this tragic conflict entails great expenditures and a corresponding sacrifice on the part of us all. We found your camp site by the Red River so I assume you have not met any other representatives of the State of Texas?"

"You're assuming right." Mark's face was deadpan.

"Then it is my duty to tell you that the State of Texas levies a tithe, one bale out of ten, from all cotton passing through her borders." Jims whipped out a limp leather book, leafed through, and spoke in a brisker tone than he had yet used. "That cotton should fetch about seventy cents a pound in Matamoros, hard gold. Won't that handle good after all that paper script? How many bales do you have?"

Mark's voice was amiable enough but his green eyes had gone hard. "I reckon I'd have to see some pretty good proof before I'd tell you that, Jims. The CSA already has its one bale out of ten. Last I heard, Texas was part of that government."

"Texas has separate and excessive expenses, Captain Morrisey." The smile stayed but small, puffy eyes were getting mean. "We must keep the roads free of bandits, support our border troops with little or no help from the central government, and we feel it only fair that those profiting from our vigilance should help pay for it." Jims paused, produced a coaxing expression and another book of small blanks. "You can pay me in cash, I'll give you your receipt, and you can proceed knowing you are paying your share to maintain this lifeline of our beloved Confederacy."

"In a pig's eye!" said Mark, cutting loose. "I'm not *Captain* Morrisey, I was a corporal and a dang good one. What's more, we have cotton agents in Missouri, too, half of them crooked, and I've heard yarns like yours before."

"Sir! You impugn my honor?"

"If you've got any. I think you're a smooth liar, Jims. Unless you can prove you're not, you don't get a red cent from us!"

Sancho dropped his bone. A pistol blossomed in his hand. Wardell Beauregard Jims suddenly held a little derringer. He must have had it strapped up his coat sleeve.

"Will this do for proof, *Corporal* Morrisey?" Jims asked politely.

None of the teamsters was near a gun. Vin, paralyzed, sat holding his plate. Mark wouldn't give in. He'd be killed.

"The money," Jims insisted, aiming at Mark while Sancho watched the rest of them. "And since you've proved troublesome I believe I'll just take all you've got."

A cackle split the air. Everyone jumped, stared at Sully who had bent double with laughter. His bald head, surrounded by its fluffy white halo, gleamed in the sun.

"Jack Sprat!" he guffawed. " 'Jack Sprat could eat no fat—' "

"Shut up!" Jims wasn't smiling. He must have been joked that way before. His voice lost its gentle, satin drawl. "Shut up, you old fool, or I'll—"

Vin hurled his plate, sent his cup after, lunging back to the wagon for his rifle. The plate struck Jims' nag, who reared, whinnying, and a veritable rain of tin cups and plates swamped the pair of swindling hijackers. Jims' gun belched futilely. The mule took off in frenzied bounds. Fighting for their balance, neither Jims nor Sancho could shoot. When they finally got their beasts under control at the edge of the woods, they turned to look back. One glance at the twenty-one teamsters, who either had guns leveled at them or were scrambling for weapons, convinced them and they rode hastily into the trees.

"Let 'em go," said Mark, chuckling. "They won't be back." He thumped Sully on the back. "Quick thinking, man! You saved my hide. You and young Vin."

Vin, collecting his cup and plate, held up the plate ruefully. Jims' bullet had claimed a victim of sorts. "Look at this hole. I sure can't eat any more gravy this trip."

"Why," grinned Mark, "you're welcome to my plate—and anything Roncky cooks, for that matter!"

Roncador snorted. "We'll see what's your tune at supper," he threatened. "All right, all of you, gather up the dishes. Plumb silly to throw 'em like that when just a few would have done as well." He went muttering to work, rinsing dust off the greasy plates, while Sully basked in the glory of his quick thinking. Jare and Vin stored the cooking supplies, and soon the train rolled out again, with only a punctured plate lost to their first Texas adventure.

KING'S RANCHO

For the next three weeks they rumbled through tall pines and gentle hills, river prairies and oak forests. Gradually the country flattened. There were fewer streams and sparser grass. Late in September they crossed the Colorado River and from then on they were in the coastal plains.

Sand and blowing winds became a constant torment. They moved only mornings and evenings but the stock couldn't live off the sere vegetation. The long canvas troughs were gotten out and painstakingly filled so not a bit of grain was spilled. There were sometimes dry camps, without water, and the suffering of the animals seemed worse than that of the men who were at least on this drive from free choice.

Mark and Roncador kept up their joking but the grins they coaxed were shorter-lived. Trig Medders lay under his wagon and neglected his team until Mark bawled him out. Grudgingly as he admitted it, Vin came to believe that Jare's fiddling helped more than anything those suffocating noons and evenings.

When there was no water and the men were too dry for singing, Jare played the fiddle anyhow, and the tunes from their green hills and bottomlands brought some peace to heat-jangled nerves. Vin would have eaten with Jare now, or taken him hunting, had the quiet boy made an advance. But Jare seemed to have forgotten Vin existed, and Vin was too stubborn to make the first move.

Sometimes he almost did, though, when the fiddle cried at night and loneliness for Darcy ached through him. Where was Darcy? He might be fighting by now, someplace Vin had never heard of. Did Mama and Pa know he'd left the train? Were they angry or worried, mostly? And how long was it going to be before he, Vin, could leave these doggoned wagons and get in on the fighting?

The further south they moved, the worse the sands became. Some days they moved a grinding, sweating four or five miles, about a third of their usual pace, which Vin had always felt maddeningly slow. To think that when they'd crossed the Red, he'd felt good and chalked it up as halfway! Vin's lips cracked as he grinned mirthlessly, and he winced, stopping the blood with his tongue. Surprised he had any blood—he felt dried to a cracklin'.

Except for stunted scrub growth, there were no trees, and they used dry chips from the animals of wagons that had gone the trail before them. In a way it was encouraging to know other humans had gone through here—and so far they hadn't found any man's skeleton though cow and mule and horse heads grinned bonily from clumps of cactus or drifted dunes.

"I don't see why anyone who's in his right mind would make this drive twice," Vin grumbled one night to Mark. They sat with their backs to the strong Gulf wind, blinking sand from their eyes and gritting it between their teeth. "I don't see why anyone would live here, either. Durn desert! Fit for nothing but dying or getting lost in!"

Mark grinned, spitting dust. "Keep that opinion to yourself when we stop at the King Ranch, Vin. I've heard Cap'n Richard sets great store by his Wild Horse Desert."

"What's that? And who's he?"

"They say the old Spaniards mapped the stretch between

the Nueces and the Rio Grande as Wild Horse Desert because
of the droves of mustangs. And King? He's about the forbid-
dingest man in this forbidding country, lad. Steamboat captain, he was, till he bought up some old Spanish grants and
moved up about forty-five miles from Corpus Christi. He owns
horses and cows that haven't been counted, and they say he
really is like a king."

"Well, he's welcome to his empire," Vin snorted. "How
come you to know about him?"

"Some men in my outfit were from Corpus Christi. They
talked about King the way the English do about Queen Vic-
toria." Mark's eyes glinted with amused remembrance. "Only,
of course, what they had to say was considerably different."

Curious, in spite of his disgust with the country and doubts
of the sanity of anyone who lived there from choice, Vin
asked, "Reckon we'll see him?"

"Maybe. We'll be at ranch headquarters in a few days, get
supplies and rest there. King's in Brownsville a lot. He and his
partner, Mifflin Kenedy, still run steamboats and have a big
finger in the cotton trade."

"Wish we could jump on a steamboat and float the rest of
the way to Brownsville!"

Mark said drily, "You'll live through worse—or die mighty
young."

Shamed, for *he* didn't have a maimed leg and some things
Mark had seen in the war must have made this drive seem
tame, Vin bit his tongue and went to help Roncador clear up
the supper things. Jare was starting a tune.

I am a poor wayfaring stranger . . .

Aren't we all! Vin snickered under his breath. When the
eating gear was stored away, he rolled up in his blankets,

back to the eternal eastern wind that came cold now at night. Captain Richard King was most heartily entitled to this place as far as Vin Clayburn was concerned!

As Mark had said, three days later they rumbled to noon camp at a creek boasting an earthen dam and trees Roncador said were *anaquas*. Unfortunately, the shade under these was already appropriated by another wagon train, one of three that must have been a few days before them on the road. The men of these trains spoke cordially enough but minded their own business.

After the stock was watered and corraled at the best remaining graze, Marked asked Vin, "Want to see the ranch headquarters enough to miss your dinner? I'm riding in to see if we can trade off our skinniest mules and if we can buy a beef."

"I'll go with you," Vin said eagerly. The idea of a big ranch, even in this desert, excited him more than he'd have confessed.

Downing fake coffee and each taking a handful of leftover biscuits, they followed the wide trail southwest.

In less than an hour they came in sight of what looked like a town. Farthest north were a line of small dwellings where Vin guessed the ranch workers lived. Stables, corrals, sheds for wagons and carriages, and a blacksmith's shop spread out towards a big stone building. By this stood a watchtower and another hotel-like building. South of this grouping rambled a low frame house with an attic and long front porch. A walkway connected the house to a stone building in the rear. Judging from the chimneys, Vin figured this separate place held the kitchen and maybe dining room to reduce the danger of fire.

"Wonder where they got enough wood to build this she-bang?" Vin mused.

"The boys from Corpus Christi said King bought most of it from the government when the army moved its post and supply depot from Corpus to San Antonio. The rest of the wood had to be brought in by boat from Florida and Louisiana." The two stopped talking as they rode into the bustle of the head-quarters.

More wagon trains, both mule- and ox-drawn, were camped in the outlying reaches, and the men from them passed among the buildings, visited the smithy, or came in and out of the big stone building, which proved to be the ranch store or commissary. As the Missourians drew rein, uncertain of where to go for information, a small, leather-encased man with a face as brown as his saddle, rode to meet them. He wore the high-peaked Mexican hat and huge silver spurs Vin had already noticed on most of the men. A business-like carbine was slung over his shoulder. The silver-studded bridle and saddle re-minded Vin of a song Darcy had picked up: *"Oh, a ten-dollar hoss and a forty-dollar saddle—"* though the ewe-necked mean-eyed, dun-colored horse would probably not fetch five dollars.

"What is it that you wish, *señores?*" asked the man in highly accented English. "I am Silvano Vargas, at your orders."

"That's right friendly of you, Mr. Vargas," said Mark. "We're with a cotton train. I'd like to see about trading some thin mules for husky ones. Is Captain King here?"

"At this moment, no, *señor*. But I have authority for trading with the caravans. Where are your beasts?"

Mark jerked his head northward. "I'll bring them later. Can you maybe sell us a beef? We sure are hungry for fresh meat."

White teeth flashed. "Now that is easy. You are camped at Tranquitas? The creek with the dam and trees?"

"I reckon that's the place."

"I'll ride out with you and instruct the *vaqueros* to butcher you a steer. Tender it will not be, *señor*. This drouth has gaunted all the creatures. But hunger makes the best sauce, is it not true?"

"We'll appreciate your trouble," Mark said. "I'm Mark Morrisey, from Missouri, and Vin Clayburn here is one of our mule-whackers."

Silvano bowed and Vin, embarrassed, ducked his head and mumbled, "Pleased-to-meet-you!" This ranchhand had the manners of what Vin dimly imagined were those of a lord or duke. Yet they fitted him natural and snug as the leather clothes.

Silvano was good as his word. Within an hour of their return to camp, two of the men called *vaqueros* brought up a black-horned steer for Mark's approval. He nodded in acceptance and they butchered it out beyond the wagons. Roncador put some of it to roasting over coals, hung enough for breakfast in a bag from a tree limb, and began to cut the rest in thin strips which he strung over a smoky fire to cure. Vin was helping him when one of the *vaqueros* jingled up and pointed at the steer's head, asking something.

Roncador nodded. Happily, the man took the head and rode over to where some of his friends waited. They skinned the head, stuck it in a tree crotch, and rode off about their work. Vin stared. Flies had already swarmed over the leavings of the carcass and it made him sick to think of them on the head.

"What'd they do that for?" he asked.

"When they get through work tonight they'll dig a hole in

the ground, bury that head, and cook it under coals. It's called *tatema*. Tastes pretty good."

"Ugh!" groaned Vin.

"You eat headcheese, don't you?" Roncador gave him a hard, almost insulted look. "Is a hog cleaner than a steer?"

"Just don't you get any fancy ideas," Vin implored, hanging the last strip of beef over the fire.

Mark and Silvano were over talking mules. Vin wandered along the creek, stopping to talk to men from the other trains. It turned out that two of them had met Wardell Beauregard Jims, and one had actually paid him the demanded tenth. The leader of the other, accosted by the third cotton agent since crossing the Texas line, had unceremoniously run him out of camp with a shotgun.

"Bunch of rogues and scoundrels," pronounced a Louisianan. "And even the honest and true-appointed ones are at cross-purposes most of the time, what with the Confederate government, the Trans-Mississippi Department, and the State of Texas all having different rules."

"Wait'll you get to Matamoros," cut in another teamster with a harsh laugh. "Bribes, rumors—oh, it's fun!"

Vin went back to his corral, ears buzzing, to see that Mark had put in a fruitful afternoon. A dozen of the worn-down mules had been replaced with animals that looked strong, if wicked, and over at the fire Roncador was roasting green coffee beans.

"Real coffee!" breathed Vin, settling down on his heels to sniff. Roncador's smile was beatific.

"Yep. Mark bought it at the ranch commissary when he went back to look over the mules. We're lucky, because they don't get it often, even with the Captain's connections."

As evening settled, tempting smells wafted from the different camps. The *vaqueros,* Silvano among them, had evidently decided to camp at Tranquitas rather than return to head-quarters, and the steer's head had been put to cooking under earth and coals.

It seemed like a holiday, among other people, and with fresh beef and coffee, supper tasted better than any Christmas or Thanksgiving dinner Vin could remember, but he mentally apologized to his mother for the thought. From the *vaquero's* camp drifted the sound of singing and Jare, as if drawn by a magnet, started off in that direction, though he was the shyest of mortals.

Darcy's fiddle was in his hand, as usual, and Vin made that an excuse to catch up with him.

"Where you going with Darcy's fiddle?" Vin demanded.

Jare seemed to rouse out of a trance. His thin cheeks reddened. "I thought I'd try to learn some songs. Darcy wouldn't mind."

Vin knew that. Darcy, in fact, would be right in the middle among these dusky leather-clad men whose voices were different and strange as the lonely winds of their Wild Horse Desert —sad, then changing to the gay thrill of a gallop and sun on the face. Vin wanted to go into that circle, too, but he had no music, no fiddle, and he hung back.

"Come on!" Jare said. For once he was impatient and showed it. "Thee can make sure I don't break the fiddle, and even thee ought to like the songs!"

They came to the shadows of the fire. Silvano Vargas saw them and came over. "Welcome, *amigos.* Will you share our *tatema?*"

"Thy songs," Jare said. "I—we'd like to listen."

Silvano's courtesy became warmth. "Then sit with us. We are honored." He spoke to the other men in Spanish. Some of them nodded and murmured greetings while others eyed the boys impassively. Soon they returned to their meal, making it a feast and an occasion, rolling black tobacco into cornshuck cigarettes, sometimes singing along with Silvano who had picked up his guitar.

De domingo en domingo
Veo la cara . . .

Vin knew it was a love song from the tender-bantering tone. He settled his chin in his hands to listen. It wasn't long till Jare was fiddling softly. How did he pick up the feel of the tune so fast? Vin wondered enviously. Even Darcy couldn't have done better.

A *vaquero* brought over some chunks of *tatema*. Vin started to refuse, but Jare took some, smiling thanks, so Vin had to gulp and do the same.

It really wasn't so bad, he decided, after the first gingerly bite. Shucks, hadn't he eaten frog's legs and pig's feet? And it was a small price to pay for this adventure, this night out of another world. Eating the *tatema* seemed to put the seal on their right to be in the firelit circle. Silvano fondled a few stray notes from his guitar and looked at Jare.

"Perhaps you would play some of your songs? It would be pleasing to us."

Vin marveled at the way Jare, as if come into his own, bent to the fiddle and played, softly first, then letting out the home-music, the Missouri tunes brought from their old countries by English and Scotch-Irish settlers, just as Silvano's songs held traces of Spain and the Moors, Montezuma, and Cortéz. Sobering and wonderful to think that behind each man stands his vast chain of ancestors, their ways and history brought to a pinpoint in each man, embodied in him for praise or shame. And like the stories Vin's mother had told him, these songs had belonged to their faraway kin and had a power to tug at the blood.

> In Scarlet town where I did live
> There was a fair maid dwellin',
> Made every lad cry, 'Well-a-day!'
> And her name was Barbary Allen.

Just starting to be a man's, Jare's voice throbbed like pain. Vin, full of nameless growings, hopes, and dreads, fairly ached. It seemed to him that all people were like this little camp—a small ring of light and cheer, singing in great darkness with winds they couldn't control blowing about them. The whole world seemed rooted in loneliness. Yet, somehow, that made the song sweeter, the light brighter and the laughter deeper.

"Sing with me," Jare whispered. "I don't remember all of *Sweet Betsy from Pike.*" Vin joined in gladly. He wanted to give the *vaqueros* a glimpse of his life as they had given him one of theirs.

> Oh, don't you remember sweet Betsy from Pike,
> Who crossed the big mountains with her lover Ike;
> With two yoke of cattle, a large yellow dog,
> A tall Shanghai rooster, and one spotted hog?

From the wagon trains, teamsters' voices took up the long story-song of the Gold Rush. Vin heard Mark's lilting roar, Roncador's wheeze. Silvano stood up and made an inviting sweep of his arms.

"*Señores,* all of you—come let us have music together!"

Just about all the men came, though some looked suspicious, most curious, and a few arrogant. These expressions melted soon, though, into the music. Jare played a while longer and then Roncador spoke to Silvano.

"Do you know *Las Mañanitas?*"

"Ah, *sí!* The Little Mornings!" Smiling, Silvano launched into the song and Roncador, evidently remembering back, joined in, groping a syllable or two behind as the *vaqueros* swelled the chorus.

So they sang, in Spanish and Missourian, till it was late and a coyote set up a mourning to the pale, silver moon.

"He sings, too," gestured Silvano.

"And it's time we slept." Mark shook hands with the *vaquero*. "Many thanks for a fine evening. We won't forget it."

"Nor we." Silvano rose. His dark eyes touched on Vin and Jare. *"Vaya con Díos, amigos."*

In camp, huddled in his blankets, Vin said to Roncador, "What did that mean? The way Silvano said good-by?"

"Go with God. You'll hear it often—provided the folks like you."

As Vin sank into dreams, it seemed plain and simple to him all at once. If everyone would get around a fire together and have music there'd be no war. He'd tell Pa and Darcy that. Of course it'd have to be a big fire. The people at the back couldn't hear and—well, maybe it wouldn't work with a big bunch, but it had done wonders tonight.

They moved out two days later. Water in the creek was so low it seemed criminal to stay longer than necessary. They rattled past ranch headquarters, using the cotton road that must have been a mile wide, the inland part used by Brownsville-bound trains, the coastside traveled by wagons coming from the Rio.

Vin was disappointed. He'd had no glimpse of Richard King, the man who had built and commanded this huge ranch. Silvano had said he was on a trip to Mexico. Maybe on their way back through—

Ever since they had camped at Tranquitas they were never far from other wagons. The King Ranch served as a cotton depot for the Confederacy and many private owners simply sold their cotton to King there and left it to him to get it to the border. Trains from all cotton-raising points west of the Mississippi converged by the time they reached the head-quarters, so dust rose thick as profanity, and this last part of the drive seemed the hardest.

"Glad it's only ninety-five miles," Roncador puffed one nooning.

"Only!" choked Vin, blinking dust from his smarting eyes.

"After over a thousand that shouldn't kill you."

At the rate of five miles a day, which was all they sometimes made in the sands, Vin wasn't so sure. He wandered over to a north-bound train, located a boy about his own age, and asked, after they had swapped names, "What are you hauling?"

"President Lincoln, of course," the boy grinned.

"No, honest. What do you bring out of Brownsville?"

"Sight more than you can get anywhere else since the Yanks took New Orleans. Come here." Importantly, the boy let Vin peer under the canvases.

"*Bean flour,*" Vin read. "*Canned goods.* Say, what is this?" Frowning, he read off another box label. "*Hollow ware.* Humph! Sure doesn't sound worth hauling all the way north."

The boy chuckled. "Hollow ware is Enfield rifles. Bean flour's gunpowder. And canned goods—shucks, that's percussion caps! The English merchants label it this way in case their ships get searched and in order to clear customs all legal and nice." He swept his hand to indicate the other wagons in his train. "We've got ammunition, guns, drugs—all the things the Confederacy has to import. The fighting men can really use these boxes."

"My brother's a soldier," Vin said. "Maybe he'll get one of these Enfields."

"Could be. Or you may haul back his good-luck rifle yourself, unless the Union takes Brownsville like old Bee is scared it will."

RIO GRANDE

Vin stared. "Bee? The Union? What are you talking about?"

"Oh, I guess you wouldn't know unless you'd talked to someone fresh out of Brownsville." The boy drew himself up a full inch in his satisfaction at spreading momentous news. "Well, see, early this summer 'Prince John' Magruder—he commands the Texas District—got nervous about Union troops in Louisiana and pulled most of our men at the border up to east Texas in case of invasion. He also replaced Rip Ford, one of the best field officers the South has, with General Bee. Ford, who was in charge at Fort Brown, is an old Texas Ranger and he knows the border and how to fight on it and handle any trouble from Mexico as well as Yankees."

"And this Bee doesn't?"

The young teamster sniggered. "His whole name is Hamilton Prioleau Bee, so what do you expect? He does his best, but he's a political brigadier general in a fighting spot."

"Where's the Union coming from?"

"There's all kinds of tales. Some say twenty thousand Yanks have been recruited in New York to invade the Rio. Others think General Banks is collecting men in New Orleans and will attack on the Gulf coast from ships."

Vin's blood raced. Maybe there was going to be some action this trip after all. "Won't Bee fight?"

"He's not got much," shrugged the boy. "A couple of siege guns, one battery of light artillery, four companies of cavalry and some home guards and mounted militia. Not over a thousand men and some of them plenty doubtful. The militia and home guard are mostly Mexican. They'd as soon fight Confederates as the Union, lots of them. And we heard that Cheno Cortina is back at the Rio and may come over with his army—try to reclaim Texas for Mexico while the North and South are fighting. Now wouldn't that top it?"

This was too much at once for Vin, too many names and facts. "Cortina?" he echoed helplessly.

"He's next in power to Ruiz who's the military governor of Tamaulipas. That's the Mexican state right across the Rio from Brownsville. Anyhow, Cortina hates gringos. Seems like back in '59 he even occupied Brownsville and killed some people. He says Texas was stolen from Mexico and he wants to get it back, at least the part along the Rio. So he sits in Matamoros, just a stone's throw from Fort Brown, and poor old Bee sees that hungry look in his green, cat eyes—"

"Dinner!" bellowed Roncador.

"Beans," groaned Vin. "Well, you make it sound interesting on the river even without the Yanks! So long and good luck."

"Same to you," called the boy. "You'll need it!"

Sharing his news at dinner, Vin concluded hopefully, "Maybe it's all rumor." Mark humphed.

"I doubt it. The Yanks have been pressuring Lincoln to stop this trade at the Rio. They know how important it is to the Confederacy even if Jeff Davis' precious cabinet doesn't."

Vin had heard his father and others complain about that before. Cotton was the only important cash crop the South had, the only thing it could exchange for munitions and drugs. It seemed only sensible to produce and sell every possible bale. But out of Davis' advisors, only one, adroit Judah P. Benjamin, urged that course. The rest of the cabinet, including President Davis, believed in another strategy.

The textile mills of Germany, France, and England relied mostly on southern cotton. In England alone twenty per cent of the working people were in the cotton-spinning industry. A shortage of cotton would drastically affect these countries. So drastically, hoped Davis' cabinet, that England at least would come into the war on the Southern side. From the start, the Confederacy had believed they would get help from Europe. Now, with their supplies exhausted and the thin foreign trickle just enough to keep them hanging on, that hope seemed the only way to victory. So the Confederacy continued its cotton policy, drawing whatever possible revenue from it while production dropped from a pre-war four million bales to 1863's five hundred thousand, and men died from lack of the drugs or weapons that hard cash could have furnished.

Mark must have been thinking of this, for his face had lost all its humor and he turned to stare south across the desert. Trig Medders spoke up, almost as if pleased to add to the gloom.

"Bee has another reason for being jumpy. I heard it from the wrangler of that other train. Seems like a man named Davis who used to be a Brownsville district attorney and judge has organized a bunch of Union sympathizers. They hang out in Mexico and cross the Rio to raid and kill. Well, shortly after Bee took command of Fort Brown, some of Davis' men came to the Texas side, killed some cotton teamsters and a well-liked Mexican. So some of the cavalrymen went to Mexico while off duty, caught Davis and his top man, Montgomery, and brought them back to Texas. They hung Montgomery and would have done the same for Davis except

Bee stopped them. He sent Davis back to Mexico with apologies for his men's violation of neutral soil, but Davis has a long memory. Bee is sure he's plotting to massacre him the first good chance—and Davis probably is, too." Trig laughed, seeming to enjoy the unhappy general's predicament.

"Whatever," said Mark, "it sounds like a troubled place."

Vin thought that was putting it mildly.

They sighted Brownsville the second of November through the blinding gusts of a wild Gulf storm. Other trains were in front of them and as they came down the wide dirt roads of the town, the sound of creaking wheels and hooves and shouts made a din that mingled with the howling wind.

In spite of this pandemonium, Vin saw the townspeople were acting strangely. Standing on the porches of houses that were mostly frame, or peering towards the southeast, the citizens seemed on guard against something. As the wagons got further into town, the streets were even more congested by townsmen driving high-piled wagons or teetering wheelbarrows. Others, arms laden, scuttled hastily among the wagons. Snatches of talk reached Vin's ears through the bewildering racket.

"Yankees!"

"Davis—renegades, thousands of 'em!"

Had it happened, then, what the boy teamster had said? Vin's heart pounded. His hands sweated on the reins. He glanced at Roncador.

"What you reckon we're heading into?"

Roncador's pepper-and-salt eyebrows met above his big nose. "No tellin', lad. At first I thought a hurricane, but it's apt to be Yankees. We'll know pretty quick, soon as Mark finds this Mr. Kraus who's supposed to handle our cotton. His office is down on the river front."

They found the line of business places with no trouble, simply by following the human current, and stopped near a building that said KRAUS & CO. A few doors down was a sign marking the office of Richard King's partner, Mifflin Kenedy. While Mark went to find their agent, Vin looked around eagerly.

Right beyond, past that stretch of wall, was Fort Brown. This side of the wall was the custom house, and there, where all the people were crowding with their household goods, must be a ferry. Women and children, clutching everything from mirrors to puppies, watched with tears or fright while their men tried to force a way for them to the Rio's bank. Roncador shook his head.

"They're all making for Matamoros. That's the story of these two towns. There's always a war or trouble going on in one of them, if not both."

"Will the Mexicans treat them all right?"

"Probably better than the Yankees. Besides most of these folks have relatives or friends in Matamoros. And it won't be long before some of the Mexicans will have to scoot across for refuge here. That's how it goes on the border."

Mark had come out in the street with a pudgy, pink little man who had yellow sidewhiskers and bristling moustache. Taking stiff, mincing steps, the stranger surveyed the wagons, turned back to Mark.

"Yes, yes, Mr. Morrisey, I know what was agreed through my contact in Missouri, but things have changed! The Yankees are landing at Brazos Island—that's only about thirty miles, and I take great risk to even buy your cotton." He waved an excited, stubby arm. "Why, the cotton yards are piled high with bales now! If the Yankees come before they can be gotten across to Mexico, I am a ruined man!" He waved his fist, on the verge of tears. "*Verdammt* bluebellies! Why must they come, fouling good business?"

Vin's stomach flopped like a landed trout. Not to sell this cotton? After the miles and miles? And Pa needed the money; all the people did, bad. He gave the reins to Roncador and slid down to join Mark.

"Can't we take it across this Rio Grande ourselves?" he asked. "I didn't drive Pa's cotton down here just to lose it!" Mark looked at Kraus.

"Aye! Supposin' we manage to get these bales to Mata-moros on our own. Would you handle the transfer to Mexican ownership and the sale for a percentage?"

"Why—" began Kraus incredulously. Then, eyeing Mark's hard blue eyes and broad shoulders, the merchant slowly relaxed. A smile widened the mouth beneath the yellow moustache. "Mister Morrisey, you get that cotton to Mata-moros and I'll do the rest. But how will you work it? The ferries are all in use."

Mark rubbed his ear. "I don't know how we'll do it but we've crossed too many rivers to let this one whip us. Want to come along?"

After just a second's hesitation, Kraus was in his office and out again, buttoning his coat. "I've an office in Mata-moros—under the name of my Mexican partner, Mercurio Suárez. We'll go there. Now you understand that with the Yankees coming no one knows whether cotton can be gotten to the foreign ships, so I can't bother with your load unless I get half the profit—"

"After we cross it to Mexico when you can't?" Mark snorted. "You can either buy the cotton outright or take

10 per cent of what we get. Don't try to make up on us for
those bales you have setting on the wharf."

"Ah," reminded Kraus, "the cotton is still on this side."

"True. So hop on a wagon and let's go!"

As soon as the wagons were out of the confused press of
the town, Mark called a halt to explain. Since Vin had talked
to the boy teamster, Bee's troubles had multiplied. Some
militia had mutinied, perhaps as part of a plan with Davis
or Cortina, and wild stories were coming from the Gulf . . .
fifty thousand Yankees were said to be landing at Brazos Island
and marching on Fort Brown. Another messenger claimed to
have sighted Davis leading a great force. And Bee's orders, in
case of Union attack, were to evacuate the fort and destroy any
cotton and supplies that might fall to the enemy.

"Now, boys," Mark finished, his red brows meeting in a
straight line of worry, "we have to move these bales across
the Rio, or we'll lose 'em. And we've got to do it tonight!"

Move it? How?

One hundred and twenty bales—sixty thousand pounds of
bulky, unwieldy cotton—this had to be gotten over a strange
river with an army on the march behind them and renegades
and bandits apt to be anywhere. If Darcy were here, he'd
have some boldly daring suggestion, and the nerve to lead
the way; but he was a long journey off. Vin looked around.

These men had to sell this cotton or be ruined, just like
the Clayburns. Why, Pa was already mortgaged up to his
ears. Everybody was eating possum these days, and it was
lucky Aunt Rachel knew how to make it taste good. *She* didn't
want to be emancipated, or Uncle Jess and their three boys.
They had their cabin by the wellhouse, their own garden and

chickens. Vin had never thought of them as slaves till he heard the word in town one day. He had been young and cruel enough to call Aunt Rachel that next time she scolded him. And had Pa ever worn him out! "They're our people," he'd said, between swishes of a hickory. "Uncle Jess' daddy came here with my father and helped him start this farm. You just remember that and don't let me hear you talk like an abolitionist!"

The despairing silence snapped Vin back to the present. Old Sully's wrinkled face seemed ready to crumple. Brother Elkanah's features might have been cleaved from granite by one of his Jehovah's thunderbolts. Plainly, they hadn't any ideas. Vin's heart sunk as he gazed at the other faces. Out of all their experiences and lives didn't they have anything to help now? Someone ought to have a notion. But they all appeared stunned, helpless.

Wild with his own impotence, bitterly angry at the Yankees, Vin clenched his hands and swallowed. It wasn't fair! The dry camps, the weeks of eating dust—to end like this?

Mark's big shoulders moved forward. He seemed to be hefting a load no one could see. "If no one's got a better fancy, let's move along this river and find a shallow place. We'll ford it before dark."

Protests broke out before his mouth closed. "There's quicksand on this river!" "We'll get stuck—be sittin' ducks for the Yankees!" "We'd get drowned!" Mark waited till the clamor ebbed.

"If anyone has a better idea," he drawled, "I'd purely admire to hear it!"

Deep silence.

"Then we'll move 'em. Trig, turn your wagon over to

your swamper and hunt a ford." Trig's chicken-hawk eyes contracted to small points.

"Yanks comin'—" He spoke thickly as if something wet and spongy was in his throat. "Yanks comin' and you aim to mess with this cotton?"

"Well, now, why do you think we left home?"

Slowly at first, then rapidly, Trig shook his head. "Not me. Not me!" He scrambled off the wagon. "I'm takin' a horse and leaving." Mark stared.

"You poor, pitiful, yellow hound," he said, when he could finally speak. "I knew you were a conscript dodger but—" He turned and spat. "Get a horse. Get some grub and your gear. And may the Lord have mercy on you for a coward."

Trig sort of faded away. No one looked at him. He was their fear made plain and ugly and they didn't want to see it.

"All right!" called Mark. "Vin, let Roncky whomp the mules and you ride scout. Let's go."

Jare helped Vin catch and saddle one of the two spare horses. Eyeing the Quaker boy closely, Vin decided that if he was panicked he didn't show it. Hands steady as Mama's on her best embroidery.

"Hope we can make it across before dark," Vin said, scanning the tomato-red sun that glinted through the veils of wind and dust.

"Thee will find a good ford. It'll be fine."

Jare spoke so cheerfully that Vin could only stare, say "Huh!" and get riding. A mighty odd boy, Jare Wheelwright, and it was getting harder to cross him off as a sissy or slightly crazed. Wagon ruts ran near the river. Vin left them to get down on the banks.

Soon he thought he'd sighted a fordable place. Clicking over the baked clay bottoms, he splashed through the shallows, made it easily to a sandbar grown with rushes and willow. He paused to look across the small stretch to the other shore.

Rio Grande. Great River.

He guessed it surely was; boundary between Texas and Mexico, safety mark for bandits or refugees from either side; scene of raids and cattle-stealing. But here it just looked like a wide, sullen brown current, not deep enough in places to cover the mud. Along the shores, though, frondy trees and bushes grew green and luxuriant even though it was November.

Leaving the sandbar, Vin followed the ripples that should indicate the shallowest depths. His horse stepped into a wash-out, swept by a hidden current, and swam for a moment, eyes glaring, nostrils distended, till its hooves struck bottom. Haunches bunching, forefeet slipping, it got its footing at last. Vin glanced back.

They had needed to swim for at least ten feet. That wouldn't do. It would be fatally easy for mules, wagons, cotton, and men to drown in one thrashing melee. Guiding his horse around, Vin took it slow, trying to judge the soupy water.

Up home, except after rains, the water was clear, greenish, bottomed by sand or white limestone. He felt sorry for people here who never got to see clean, pretty water that cooled you just to see it. Of course, after Wild Horse Desert, mud looked beautiful, anything that was halfway damp . . .

How about that place?

Vin rode into it slow. Seemed to dance right lively and it was shallow at both sides. The horse lost one foot, shifted weight and regained its balance. Water rose to the stirrups, to the horse's belly. Now . . . for a few seconds, the horse swam, then struck bottom again, swiftly moved into the shallows near the Mexico bank.

Not too bad. Vin tried several other places, but that one proved the best. With the sun almost down, there was no time to hunt for a perfection one seldom found anyhow when it came to fords. Vin rode back to where he could signal the train, told Mark of his find.

"Good," nodded Mark. "We can do it—hitch two sets of teams to each wagon, so only a few mules at once will be off their feet and the others can hold 'em. We may wet some of the bales but that's better than losing them all."

"I—I believe," quivered Mr. Kraus, "that I prefer to ride horseback."

Jare said, "You can go across on mine. I'll take the last horse and use him bareback." Kraus made it over while the teamsters worked feverishly against the coming darkness, rearranging teams till the five lead wagons had twenty mules each and the rear ones had none.

"Here we go," exhorted Mark, swirling out his whip so it cracked like a pistol. "Vin, you ease alongside and help any critter that starts floating off."

Rattling down the bank with the heavy wagon, the mules slowed as they hit the muck. Straining, they reached the water while the wheels ground and splattered mud and water.

"Gee up there! Whoo-ee! Gee—gee!"

The lead team hit the deep part, lost footing, churned frantically, rearing their heads, lurching the next team after them. Vin kneed in fast, caught the head harness of the near mule, and dragged him to solid bottom. Whirling to get the next one, Vin saw Jare had him.

"Thanks," he panted.

Jare flashed a grin. "I work for the train, too."

They both did, for the next good while, catching the lead

mules of each wagon and hauling them to safety, riding along and helping where needed.

As the wagons lumbered up the other bank, their drivers got them to level ground and began unhitching the teams for their return trip to get the remaining wagons. As soon as five wagons had crossed, the teamsters, aided by Vin and Jare, brought the teams back to Texas. The last wagon crossed in the dark, but the ford was so familiar by now that all went safely.

Soaked, muddy, dog-weary, the men looked at each other. Vin couldn't see but he reckoned all their smiles were relieved and proud as his. Not a mule had been lost, not a bale of cotton.

"Now," said Mark to Kraus, "in the morning you can show us into town!"

YANKEES!

During breakfast before dawn, Mr. Kraus spoke wonderingly. "I wish I had you men working for me. Not a thing would I lose to the Yankees!"

"They wouldn't get anything off me," Mark said grimly, "if I had to burn it." The merchant winced at the word.

"That is what will happen to all the cotton in the yards if it can't be moved by steamer. *Ach!* What sorrow, what misfortune!"

"It's something to be alive," Roncador observed.

"True, sir, true. Your intelligence is piercing as your coffee."

Mark straightened, putting down his cup. "We'll hook the teams up and get rolling. Ride with me, Mr. Kraus, and show the way."

In the Matamoros shipping district, they pulled into a cotton yard. Kraus hopped down and said briskly, "Let's see the condition of the cotton, Mr. Morrisey, and then I'll make you my best figure."

As the teamsters unloaded the heavy bales, Kraus went about checking them. When at last all the bales were stacked and Vin and the others rested, panting, Kraus opened a small notebook, did some computing, and smiled at Mark.

"One hundred and twenty bales, but twenty are damp."

A gasp went up from the men. Roncador sniffed through his flattened nose, found one dampish bale, and pulled past the wet lint to show the dry fluff immediately beneath it. "A good dew tonight could wet it this much! You goin' to argue over what may be your last cotton?"

"Mmmmf." Kraus walked around and around the bales till Vin was ready to scream. "I don't know when and if I can get this lightered out to the foreign ships but you've shown great enterprise and I'll try to help. Thirty cents a pound."

Mark's eyes got stormy as the clouds above them. "Listen. If the Yanks take Brown it'll be a long spell, if ever, before cotton gets to you again. What I have is worth more than it ever has been. I'm bound you'll find a way to get it on the ships. Eighty-five cents a pound or I'll take it elsewhere."

"You rob me," Kraus moaned. "Me, a ruined man, a patriot—"

Mark turned. "Load it up, boys."

"Wait!" Kraus grabbed Mark's arm and held it tight. "Maybe—it is ridiculous—but seventy cents?"

"Get along with it, men," ordered Mark.

"Yes, yes, then—it is eighty-five but for the one hundred dry bales only!" Bent as if with real physical pain, Kraus went inside the frame building beyond the yards. When he came back, he carried a hamper.

"Here," he said lavishly.

Suspiciously, Mark opened the wicker top. He brought out a handful of rustling paper. Confederate paper money—worth about twenty to one in gold. Mark stuffed it back.

"Any more jokes?"

Kraus practically wept. But when he came back from the office again, he carried bags that jingled. He counted out the coin as if each piece were wrung from him, but when he finished, there was $42,500 in hard money. Pa's share would be over four thousand—more than they had dared hope. This would clear most of their debts, put in a new crop. And they had snatched this out of the teeth of the Yankees. Kraus looked up and sweat dripped from his moustache and sidewhiskers.

"Excuse me. Good-by. I must see about getting this cotton moved." He bustled off, and if he was at a loss about how to proceed, he didn't show it. Mark grinned.

"He'll have that cotton Europe-bound and his profit cinched before an hour's up. But we did fine, too. Now any of you want your share of this money can have it, or I'll keep it in my wagon."

Everyone decided to let Mark have the responsibility. They turned the wagons around and rattled fast out of the Mexican town, past the acacias and trees Roncador said grew strange fruit called oranges, past the wattled huts, and the imposing walled dwellings with date trees rising above their closed gardens.

With empty wagons, they could move at a good clip, and the fording was comparatively easy. On the Texas shore they stopped and voted on what to do next. Mark thought they should swing back to Fort Brown and see if there was anything they could do.

"If Bee decides to fight and wants volunteers," he said, "I'd not mind another crack at the Yanks."

High spirits ran through the men after their feat with the cotton. No one argued that they'd be risking their money. When Mark called for the hands of those in favor of going to the fort, every man raised his. Soon they were urging the mules along the outskirts of Brownsville, avoiding the mad confusion that had grown worse since last night.

As they entered Fort Brown unchallenged, passing the infantry barracks, parade ground, and guardhouse, Vin decided that the military were as utterly demoralized as the civilians. The lack of any plan or final authority showed in the worried or frightened faces of the militia and troopers who rushed aimlessly about.

Mark halted the train, evidently trying to find out where to report. A captain, with a desperate air of trying to maintain some kind of order, strode up.

"Volunteering for transport? Just turn there by the officers' quarters and bear for the Quartermaster's storehouses."

"Well," said Mark, "we had kind of hoped if there was a fight—"

As if he had said it a hundred times and was both ashamed and weary of it, the officer snapped, "General Bee's orders are to evacuate the fort and destroy all cotton and supplies we can't move first."

"But—how about those people in Brownsville? You're not going to help them at all?"

"This is war. We do what headquarters tells us."

Mark leaned forward. "Just what is known for sure about these Yankees?"

"Yesterday morning a courier brought word that Union ships were off the bar. The general sent two cavalry details out to scout. Meantime, all sorts of wild stories are coming in. All I can say is we're evacuating, so get your wagons over to the Quartermaster." Before he could be questioned further, the harassed captain swung up the street.

At the Quartermaster's, Mark turned his wagon over to his swamper and climbed down. "Go ahead and get loaded," he said. "And Sully, you go to the wagon park and see if we can get some grain for the mules. What we brought from home is about used. I'm going to hunt up General Bee."

"Off to try to talk the General into putting up a scrap," Roncador grinned. "Luck to him—but I doubt he'll get anywhere." He looked at the stormy sky, the roiling blacks and purples toward the Gulf. "If those troops didn't land yesterday, they probably can't till this storm lets up—and even if they do, their ammunition will be soaked. Disembarking troops can't fight, especially with wet powder."

"Yeah," muttered the sergeant who had come to direct their loading. "If old Rip Ford was here, he could take a hundred men and shove the whole kit and caboodle into the water. He wouldn't be sitting here sending out spies, you bet!"

Soldiers and teamsters worked together, packing supplies into the wagons while already-crammed ones lumbered past, leaving the fort. In half-an-hour, Vin glanced up to see Mark limping heavily along the lagoon that bordered the storehouses.

Without a word, the big man started hefting boxes and bundles. "What happened?" burst out Vin when he could no longer bear the suspense.

"Sure and that Bee belongs in a bonnet—and petticoats!" growled Mark explosively. "Says his orders are to save the supplies and get out, and that's what he's going to do! So while he runs and Prince John Magruder strips the border of troops, the Union moves in and closes the South's last port. Our last way of getting cotton out and supplies in!"

"If old Rip were just here—" wished the sergeant who had mentioned him before.

"Sure," said another trooper savagely, "but they've got him pushing pencils at the Conscription Bureau! Him, who should have been made a general!"

As the loading proceeded and men came and went, rumors came thicker and wilder. Yankee cavalry had crossed at Boca Chica, were sweeping across Palo Alto Prairie towards the fort . . . E. J. Davis at the head of ten thousand drunken

Negroes was marching to burn Brownsville to the ground and put his enemies to death. They were sighted only three miles from town . . . They'd be here in an hour!

A Mexican home-guardsman who was loading shrugged philosophically. "Yankees, Davis, Cortina—if it is the time of destruction, it is the time, and who can escape it? Men die, the Rio stays. And *el otro lado.*"

"What's that?" Vin asked.

"The other side. Mexico for Texans, Texas for Mexicans."

A trooper laughed. "That's what soldiers and sheriffs get told here when they're hunting someone. That he's on 'the other side', and if he's smart he will be."

"For a little while," smiled the Mexican, with a measuring gesture of his thumb, "till authority changes. That is like the current of the Rio; always there is one, but it changes. If the Yankees come, they will as surely go."

That was all very well, Vin thought, if it hadn't been for what they would do first. The wagons were almost loaded, even to the grain Sully had obtained, when the captain they had met earlier hurried up.

"Move out!" he called. "General Bee's orders! Take the way to the King Ranch!"

"What about the rest of this stuff?" Mark asked, pointing at the heaped supplies.

"We'll have to burn it—the cotton, too! Now move out! There's going to be eight thousand pounds of gunpowder blow up here pretty quick!"

The officer moved on amid the pandemonium that had possessed the fort. Torches were being set to the sheds and buildings, to the unloaded supplies. From the river came tremendous rattling as the siege guns were hauled and dumped in the water. Vin and the others hitched their teams to the wagons and hustled the mules from the growing smoke, the stench of burning cotton.

What a waste! The bales hauled so far and worth such a price going up in billows of flame and smoke, the materials so desperately needed by the South burning in the warehouses, the fort laid in ruins—but the worst was in the town, in the streets leading to the choked ground about the ferry. The sloping road was jammed with families, heaps of furniture, bedding, clothes, everything from iron bedsteads and stoves to pianos and family portraits.

The wagons, though not in the thick of the press, had to go slowly, grinding to a stop often as refugees clambered past, their arms full, bundles over their backs. Down by the river, men with pistols were forcing passage for their families on the ragtag assortment of skiffs and boats.

"They're charging five dollars gold to take a person across on those leaky old rafts," one man fumed. "But with that coward Bee running, what can we do?"

Children wailed and whimpered, men swore, and women stared Gulfward with terror in their eyes.

Vin, urging his mules along, felt sick. This wasn't his idea of war. War was lean young men like Darcy, gallantly uniformed, swinging sabers and charging into gunfire. War was bugle notes and flags, General Lee on Traveler, Jackson standing like a stone wall. War was battle between armed men; not this despair of an abandoned town, of people left defenseless because they weren't strategically important. War wasn't—

But it was! Yes, it was waste and greed and panic, gutted homes, old people and babies without a roof. Kraus making his profit and Wardell Beauregard Jims. Then up ahead, Mark's voice rang out, and Vin knew there was more than this—hard fights and sacrifice, comradeship and honor between men. But how could something made by people be so many things? Maybe that was why, exactly, war showed many sides. It *was* made by people and it pushed them to the extremes, proud or shameful, that they were capable of.

At last they were out of Brownsville and on the road north. Vin, driving the last wagon, heard distant cries muffled in a drum of hooves. Mounted soldiers swept past, raising dust, and halted up by Mark's lead wagon while Vin blinked grit from streaming eyes and Roncador sneezed and raged. An officer's voice floated back to them.

"You're moving too slow. Jettison some of your load so you can keep up."

Vin could almost see the deliberate motion of Mark's red head. "We'll make it."

"But we're to escort you teamsters to the King Ranch!"

"Never you mind," boomed Mark. "Tell the general we'll be along directly—with everything we loaded at Fort Brown."

Giving up, the troopers went on, catching up to the wagons that had left the fort ahead of the Missourians. Bee must be up there, too. Orders or no, Vin thought this would be an awfully hard thing to explain later. He himself felt guilty and shamed though he was doing the only thing he could.

About sunset they came to a brackish, reed-grown creek, corraled, and camped. They were only about five miles out of Brownsville and as the night deepened, they could see a far red haze. The fort was still burning. In the distance ahead glowed the campfires of the other wagons and the soldiers.

"They must have dumped some of their load or they couldn't have traveled that fast," Mark brooded during supper. "Well, we're going to make it with what we left with, at least! It's not enough the South is short of supplies and won't be able to get any more unless some new route to Mexico works out—Bee has to destroy all that stuff!"

"You think the Yankees will follow us?" worried Sully.

"I doubt it. It'll take 'em a while to get the town straightened out and learn what happened." Mark dragged angrily on his pipe till his teeth must have scarred the stem. "I'm betting that Bee damaged Brownsville worse than the Yankees will, unless some revenge-hunter like that Davis really is in charge. Yankees, human-speaking, aren't much different from us, it's just their ideas. One brought me a drink when I was wounded—and he had to dodge bullets to do it." Standing up, Mark stretched.

"From here to the King, we'll push hard, so let's get some sleep. We'll post night guards. Volunteers?"

"I'll take first watch," offered Jare.

"And you can roll me out when you get tired," said Vin. In minutes the train had bedded down and there seemed to be only seconds between Roncador's first blasting snore and Jare's hand on Vin's shoulder, rousing him.

Stumbling up, Vin doused some of the mucky water on his face, made a round of the camp. He was too sleepy to trust himself to sit down, or even stand still very long. Prowling over to the campfire's grayed embers, he poured a cup of coffee and blessed the King commissary for the change from the rye-sweet potatoes-corn-or-meal imitations. The drink, lukewarm and bitter though it was, sharpened his senses. He started a second tour of the corral, stopped at a slight sound.

Labored breathing, the crunch of steps. Vin faded behind a wagon. A shadow was moving down the road, a small humped shadow. It was weighted heavily from the painfully slow progress it made, and didn't seem very dangerous. Vin decided to watch a minute before challenging.

Approaching the nearest wagon, the figure put down something and seemed to feel under the canvas. Vin stepped up beside it.

"Wait a minute," he warned.

Knocked almost flat by the impact of a springing body, he grappled with a wiry frantic strength which he immediately knew was much less than his—this must be a young boy. Pinioning the hands, Vin avoided bare, kicking feet, pried up the face. It was too dark to see more than a vague oval under the peaked Mexican hat.

"Now, boy," panted Vin, "what's the idea?"

More kicks, a stamp on his foot. Vin gave his captive a shake. "Say! Speak English? Savvy American?" The head, hat and all, butted at his ribs.

"Speak English?" choked the prowler in an outraged gasp. "A good deal better than you, bad-smelling, rough-handed gringo!"

Startled out of his wits, Vin let go as if burned. The voice was feminine—angry, young, oddly accented. "Why—what were you doing? Poking into our wagon—?"

"*Estúpido!* How else should I escape the Yankees?"

"You're from Brownsville?"

"As any *tonto* could guess!"

Vin held on to his temper though hot blood warmed his cheeks. "You're lucky you didn't get shot and you're wastin' those high words on me because I don't understand 'em! Come along and talk to our captain."

"What's to talk about?" The girl bent to pick up the heavy object she had set down by the wagon. "I will take my sewing machine and go."

"Where?" Vin demanded. "You can't walk to the King Ranch with that—whatever that contraption is. Let's talk to

Mark. We'll help you if we can. After all, we're from the same country."

She shook her head. "You don't live on the Rio. Or even in Texas."

"This is no time to fight a new war. Come on!"

After a minute she seemed to decide that, though determined, he wasn't vicious. She turned and walked ahead of him. Vin located Mark and knelt, speaking softly in his ear. No use waking up the whole train.

"Mark, there's a girl here—run away from Brownsville. You've got to talk to her."

"Oh, I do?" growled Mark, rolling over, rubbing his eyes. Then he sat bolt upright. "A *girl?*"

"That's right." In spite of his own worry, Vin almost laughed.

Mark shucked off his blankets. Sighting the girl, he crossed to her and bowed. "Mark Morrisey, ma'am, at your bidding." The big wagonmaster bent as close as he politely could— trying to see if she were pretty.

Vin figured she was; either that or dirt homely to have such a tongue. *"Pretty girls and plain ones can act feisty,"* Mama used to say, *"for in either case it doesn't matter."*

"I'm Estrella Riley," said the girl graciously, accepting Mark's courtliness. "This—this *boy* of yours is treating me like a thief."

"When you sneak around people's wagons, what do you expect?" Vin demanded.

The others ignored him. "Let's just step out here where we don't have to shout over Roncador's snoring," suggested Mark. They all moved a way from the sleeping crew. "Now, then, Miss Riley, tell us what we can do to help you."

"When General Bee left the fort, he also left eight thousand

pounds of powder which exploded and sent debris everywhere. It even caved in part of the Matamoros customs house.
The falling brands acted like torches—they set fire to the
buildings along the river and showered down on the people
and goods at the ferry. I had carried my sewing machine down
there, trying to cross to Mexico, but when the fire hailed down
on us, I ran back."

"Don't you have any folks?"

"My parents are dead and my father's kin are in Ireland;
my mother's in Mexico City. For the past year, since my
mother died of yellow fever, I have lived alone and sewed
for a living."

"But—neighbors? Friends?"

"My parents lived together against the world's opinion
since their religions and race were different. They taught me
not to need anyone."

"Now you do."

She tossed her head. "Truly? And what could those who
cannot help themselves do with me if I did beg them? *Ay,*
no, Señor Morrisey! I must manage for myself. The town was
filling with drunkards, riffraff from both sides of the river.
I pushed my hair into an old *sombrero* and left town, hoping
to catch up with the wagons." Mark was still a long time.
When he spoke it was with reluctance.

"Miss Estrella, the Yankees aren't so bad. Let me send
you back on a horse. You'll be better off in a place where
people know you and will pay some mind than wandering
around the wagon routes."

"Yankees have blue bellies and are beasts! They kill
babies and bayonet women!"

Gently, Mark said, "I've seen lots of 'em, Miss, and they

look just like us and mostly act that way. You've heard a bunch of fool stories!"

"I won't go back to the Yankees! I won't, I won't!" She began to cry, all her composure broken. "My mother remembered them from when Taylor built Fort Brown during the last war. They were awful!"

Mark shifted from his bad leg, thinking. Vin was glad this problem wasn't his to decide. "We'll take you to the King," Mark said finally. "You can stay there till we see what happens in Brownsville, or maybe Captain King can arrange something for you." Estrella Riley thought it over. At last, she nodded.

"Very well. And now I would like to sleep."

As if there were nothing left to worry about, she marched back to the wagon where her sewing machine waited. Vin stared at Mark. Mark stared at Vin. Then Mark laughed.

"Let's scrape her up some blankets. Then you sleep till morning. I'm too rattled for it myself! If Bee had her spirit we wouldn't be running from Yankees!"

KING'S JUSTICE

For once Vin woke to a sound other than Roncador's thunder on a skillet. A pleasant sound. Laughter. Sweet and tinkly rather than the bellowings usually heard around camp. Raising on an elbow, Vin blinked towards the sound.

As he saw the poncho-wrapped figure by the cookfire, memories of last night filled him with a shock that wiped all sleepiness from his brain. So that was Estrella Riley!

Her cream, orange and brown poncho was belted with silver conchos and fell to her knees where leather pants like those *vaqueros* wore took over. Slim, small feet were in tooled leather sandals. The big hat was gone and black hair tossed curling in the breeze. As if she felt Vin's stare, she turned.

For a moment he looked into eyes, as blue as the Rio sky, beneath black eyebrows that arched up like an eagle's wings. Vin jerked his head in embarrassed greeting. She frowned, gave him a doubtful nod, and went back to helping Roncador and chattering.

Vin fled to water his mules. Most of the men were up before him and as they gathered for breakfast after harnessing up, he took some comfort from the way all of them, even Sully and Brother Elkanah, couldn't keep their eyes off the girl.

And Jare—! Vin snickered into his coffee as the wrangler tripped over himself while the girl filled his plate. Jare looked like he'd been hit in the stomach and couldn't catch his breath.

They traveled till almost noon, the girl riding in the wagon Trig Medders had abandoned to his swamper. Since there was little graze and no water, the nooning was more a stop in an inferno than a rest.

It was too bad, Vin thought, noticing how the girl brightened and raised the men's spirits, that she didn't have the same effect on the mules who needed it most. Snuffing grain from the canvas troughs, the poor animals could hardly swallow the dry feed. And it was going to be this way most of the miles to the ranch. Early in the afternoon, they pushed on.

The wagons ahead were long since out of sight. As the day wore on, the Missourians began to see why. Heaps of blackened cotton marked the road. To speed up the wagons, Bee must have ordered part of their cargo destroyed.

That wasn't all. Here and there, wheel tracks would lead off the rutted way, go to some growth of brush or gully, and then swing back. Vin was almost curious enough to investigate when he saw Estrella spring from the slow-moving wagon and follow one of the detours.

She stopped by a big wall of prickly pear, disappeared around it. By the time Vin was having to turn sideways to watch, she came in sight again, moving swiftly, lightly, even in the yielding sand. She held a tuft of white fleece in her hand.

"Ah," breathed Roncador. "Some sly teamster cached his bales instead of burning them. Hopes to go back for 'em when there's time, or just plain couldn't stand to burn them."

In camp that night, Vin noticed that Estrella was busy with a pencil and Mark's account book, making what looked like a map.

"What is that?" he asked, when he could no longer control his bafflement. Her eyebrows rose almost to unruly black curls.

"I'm marking the cotton caches," she explained with patient scorn. She could have been speaking to a not especially bright child.

"Why do you want to do that?"

After an amazed glance, she spoke slowly, carefully, as if making allowances for him. "I shall see, if no one else does, that the cotton doesn't stay here and rot. Men are great wasters. If they were not so terrible these wars of yours would be like nothing so much as a child's game where whoever destroys the most wins."

Vin had felt much the same at Fort Brown, but he felt bound for the honor of men to say snubbingly, "Well, Miss Riley, if it weren't for men, you'd be in a fix right now! There aren't any women driving these wagons, you'll notice."

"If it weren't for men I wouldn't be here and I wouldn't have lost everything but my sewing machine and these old clothes of my father's!"

Roncador chortled. "She's got you there, Vin."

With as much dignity as he could command, Vin stalked away, but he felt as if he were slinking off in defeat. After supper, when Jare played the fiddle, Estrella sat by the fire and it was as though the music was for her. *What had got into everybody?* Vin wondered grouchily. Women certainly didn't belong on wagon hauls!

Rolling, urging on weary, thirsty teams, watching from dust-bitten eyes the sameness of the cotton-tagged brush along the road. This was the fourth day out of Brownsville. By hard pushing they had made about sixty miles, the last forty of which had been marked with burned or cached bales.

"Boy howdy!" Roncador said more than once, as the mules kicked up charred fleece. "Bee's going to feel mighty foolish if the Yanks don't chase after us. Folks will remember this about him for a long time."

"Look at those cattle over there," Vin pointed. They were the small, sharp-horned creatures he had glimpsed often. "Reckon they belong to anybody?"

"Them?" Roncador hitched a shoulder. "Those are *cimar-rones*, wild ones. They're like mustangs—belong to anybody that can catch 'em, unless they're already branded or fenced. Unless they're bred with meatier stock, they're hardly worth the trouble. For, lad, they are mean! When I was through here with Zach Taylor, danged if some of them didn't charge the whole army. We ran, too, you bet!"

Vin laughed. "Don't blame you. But they'd be fresh meat which we could sure use. Think I'll try to bag one at noon."

"Just be certain he's not branded or ear-marked," Roncador warned. "We're on the King Ranch now."

At noon, after the mules had been unharnessed to find such graze as they could, Vin went to saddle a horse, said to the question in Jare's face, "I'm hunting a *cimarrón*. Want to join me?"

"I'm not much of a shot."

"Well, I am. And you can fiddle for Miss Estrella Riley tonight. Come on and give her ears a rest."

Reddening, but looking pleased, Jare slung his saddle on his horse, and they angled west towards some ridges covered with tangled brush and mesquite.

"If they have any sense," reasoned Vin aloud, "they'll be in those trees, resting in the shade till it gets cooler."

"And if we had any sense, we'd be under the wagons!"

Vin hooted. "You won't say that when we're eating steak."

They rode into the rolling little hills, really just sand dunes held down by scrub growth. A thicket of sizable mesquite came in sight. "Look!" cried Vin, pleased. "There's a trail leading into that grove—sort of a tunnel. Bet the cattle made it and some are back in there right now."

"And I bet they won't like it if we go crowdin' in."

"Then," snorted Vin, "we'll beg their pardon!"

Ducking to avoid the low-hanging thorn canopy, he led the way. It was almost dark as a hall inside, a hall with olive green walls and ceiling. The thicket was threaded with white paths leading toward the middle where they joined at a hole. Cracked mud showed it had once held water which attracted the wild path-makers.

"Shucks," said Vin in disappointment. "If there's no water, maybe they don't come here any more."

The boys moved on from this wide spot into another corridor, holding their arms and legs close to their bodies to avoid the thorns. The tunnel made a sharp curve. Vin, still leading, went around it to confront red eyes glaring up from between a pair of curved prong horns.

Vin's horse pranced back, bumping into Jare's who fidgeted and wheeled into another tunnel. The *cimarrón* charged. Vin, acting more by instinct than plan, backed his horse into the central clearing, reining it sharp to the side.

Churning up white dust, the *cimarrón* thundered past. Vin pulled out his Sharps, worked the trigger guard loading lever that opened the breech, loaded, and fired as the animal weighted itself to a stop, whirled, and spun back to attack.

Vin's bullet took it in the head but it came straight on and this time there was no handy opening down which to dodge.

Whickering, his horse reared, plunging Vin into ripping, lacerating thorns. Battling it down, he clubbed the Sharps, brought it down on the nearing horned head though he knew it was useless.

The *cimarrón* veered suddenly, wheeling around. Jare had flung himself from his horse and caught the wild bull's tail, kinking it the way Vin had often done in Missouri to get a lazy or sullen cow to its feet. Vin reloaded.

"Run!" he yelled. "Get down one of the trails!"

Jare let loose and tore down a tunnel. The bull went after him as Vin got in a sideshot. It must have hit the heart or lungs; the *cimarrón* took two more bounds, fell to its knees, slowly folded over them, small eyes glazing.

Just to make sure, Vin stayed in the saddle a minute. He was so shaky just then he probably couldn't have stood anyway.

"Get him?" Jare called.

"Between us, we did." Vin wiped sweat from his eyebrows as Jare came in sight. "Thanks, Jare. You were a fool to try that, but I'd have been a goner if you hadn't."

"Well," explained Jare seriously, "I couldn't shoot for fear of hitting thee, and I'd probably have missed. But I knew I could grab his old tail!" He looked up and suddenly they were both laughing; the air reached deeper into them than it ever had and the light was sweeter because they were still alive. Vin climbed down, tossed his reins over a limb.

"Boy, I'm steak hungry! Let's get this critter to camp."

They couldn't manage the whole carcass so they butchered in the clearing, discarding the waste parts, placing the meat in the hide. This they made into a kind of hammock-container. Fastening one end of the hide to each of their saddles, they guided the fractious horses out of the thicket before they

mounted and rode abreast. The horses didn't like the smell
of fresh blood or the odd burden, but the boys steadied them
with firm hands and voices.

"Fresh meat for supper and breakfast," Vin said, elated.

"Yep," said Jare happily. His voice changed. "Say—over
the ridge! A bunch of riders."

In a few minutes the dozen horsemen closed around them.
From their leather clothes they could have been either bandits
or *vaqueros*.

"*Qué es esto?*" demanded the leader, a graying man with
hooked nose and a fierce mouth. His carbine seemed as much
a part of him as his arm, and his men handled their weapons
as if they were well used to them. They had made a half
circle around Vin and Jare—*like hawks set to pounce on a
pair of pullets,* Vin thought, a cold chill working up his spine.

He shook his head. "No savvy."

Then Jare, to Vin's gaping wonder, spoke in Spanish, halt-
ingly but evidently getting his meaning across. The leader
scowled. He rode close and peered at the butchered *cimarrón,*
glared at both boys, and rapped out a sentence. Vin caught
the word "King".

Jare replied earnestly, but he wasn't making any headway
with the *vaquero* who shook his head, pointed at the hide,
and said a few grim words.

"What's he want?" Vin asked Jare.

"He claims we killed a King cow."

"But it's unbranded—out here doin' no good to anybody!"

Jare shrugged. "That doesn't seem to signify. Appears anything that breathes on Wild Horse Desert is King's. And we're
not getting shot right this minute on account of Captain King
himself will be along directly. He and this crew were eating

dinner when they heard our shots, so these men came ahead while their boss cleaned his plate."

"Oh." Vin couldn't think of anything else to say.

Surely it couldn't happen—two boys shot for one old, wild bull? But—a glance at the wild circle around them reminded Vin forcefully that he was in a world different from his home; a place where King's word was absolute as any medieval lord's had ever been. He searched the hard, sun-blackened faces, wondering if any of these men had been with Silvano the night they all sang and he had thought the music could make peace. What a crazy notion that had been!

The horses didn't like their nearness to the carcass and kept fidgeting and shying. Flies hovered about the hide, stinging the boys impartially, and the sun beat down. Carelessly alert, the *vaqueros* watched. Vin and Jare sweated. The leader's eyes raised. A sort of relaxation spread through his men. They moved back, forming wings about their prisoners. Over the ridge came a horseman in black, his broad shoulders bent forward slightly, perhaps from spending much time hunched over his reins.

Riding forward, the *vaquero* chief swept off his hat, explained the boys with a wave of his carbine, and drew aside for his master to view the catch.

This had to be Richard King. He rode closer. Vin found himself looking into pale eyes in a sunburned face framed by black beard and hair, a black hat turned almost gray from dust. He looked about Mark's age, in his late thirties. As his eyes bored into Vin's, it took all the boy's courage not to flinch.

"Well," came a deep-chested voice, "you're pretty young to hang for cattle-thieving, but then you're pretty young to be doing it."

"It wasn't branded, sir." Vin swallowed but his voice still climbed and cracked. "It's a *cimarrón* and didn't belong to anyone."

White teeth showed in the mass of beard. "Lad, what doesn't belong to somebody else, belongs to me. Automatically." The *vaquero* said something, pointing to the mesquite thicket.

"Felipe says we can hang you right over there," King said pleasantly.

"We're with a cotton train," Vin protested desperately. "It's nooning right over on the Brownsville road. Mark Morrisey will tell you we're not thieves!"

"Morrisey?" King frowned, tasting the name. "You come through here several weeks ago while I was gone, buy a beef from Silvano?"

Vin nodded.

Reining his horse about, King said, "We'll hunt up your wagonmaster. I can't have cotton freighters living off my beef, but I want to be fair." He tossed some directions in Spanish to the *vaqueros* who looked like disappointed watchdogs. It seemed to Vin that Felipe gave his neck a last longing look as the *vaqueros* fell in behind him and Jare.

The Missourians saw them coming and Mark and Roncador came out to meet them. "I'm Richard King," said the ranchman. "These boys belong with you?"

"Yes." Mark's quick eyes took in the meat-packed hide, the boys, and the *vaqueros'* carbines. "Something wrong? I'm Mark Morrisey, in charge here."

"Last time you ate a Santa Gertrudis beef, Mister Morrisey, you paid for it. What made your teamsters think times had changed?"

Mark strode up to examine the hide. "There's no brand on this critter. He's no more yours than the birds flying over or the jackrabbits." King smiled. His tone remained good-natured but his eyes were hard.

"That's your opinion, sir. But on my land, it's my opinion that counts. I couldn't prove ownership in a court of law—but then where is a court?"

Estrella Riley came out from the wagons. The perpetual wind whipped her hair back like a mustang's mane and her eyes, strange blue, pierced into the big captain.

"We're on your land, too, *señor,* but you don't own us! You don't claim the wind and sun, do you? Well, the *cimarrones* and mustangs are not yours, either, until you brand them!"

"Mmmm?" choked King, startled. He bent his gaze on the girl, knitted black brows relaxing a trifle though his voice was stern. "And who are you, *señorita?* A lawyer, perhaps, brought along as protection for thieves?"

She gave him an unwavering stare. "Your wife is the daughter of a minister, Captain King. You have heard the laws of God. Aren't you afraid to claim all living things that cross your land?"

"Well!" mused the captain. The big hand over his beard couldn't muffle the laugh that erupted from it. "If you're going to bring my wife and the Reverend Hiram Chamberlain into it, I guess I must retreat. Eat that stringy beef and my blessings on your digestion!" He turned to Mark. "Pardon my curiosity. But when did freighters start taking women along?"

"You haven't heard about Fort Brown?"

King's hand bit into the reins. "What's to hear?"

"Union troops landed at Brazos Island to attack Fort Brown. General Bee's orders were to evacuate and destroy what he couldn't move. Surprised you haven't met him. He ought to be almost a day ahead of us and his trail's marked with burned cotton."

"Burned cotton?" King's words took on the explosiveness of an oath.

"He sent all the wagons he could get together towards your ranch with supplies. Some had cotton. And I guess when he's met a train headed south to Brownsville, he's made them dump part of their freight and scurry back north with him." Mark gave King a grim smile. "I reckon, Captain, that your ranch ought to be a right interesting place just now."

King seemed to have to let it all soak in before he could speak. "I've been gone from headquarters a week. We've been chasing bandits west of here. You—you mean to say Bee left Fort Brown—the cotton route—to the Yanks without a fight?"

"He left Brownsville panicked with the people trying to get to Matamoros," Estrella Riley said bitterly. "Everything was burning along the waterfront, including your partner's office." King's jaw clamped in rigid planes.

"—when I see that Bee!" was all that emerged plainly. He looked down at Estrella.

"I take it you fled Brownsville, Miss? You're joining your family somewhere?"

She shook her head. "I'm going to find a place where I can make my living. I managed to save my sewing machine, and I make nice things." Mark loomed protectively by the girl.

"Miss Estrella hasn't any close kin, Captain. I was hoping you might arrange passage for her to some safe town."

"She can just stay at the Santa Gertrudis," King said. "My wife would appreciate her company, and Lord knows we could sure find plenty of sewing without looking past our own children. Would you consider it, Miss—Estrella, is it?"

"Estrella Riley," she supplied. "I will certainly think on it, Captain King."

"Do more than that," he boomed. "I'd like to know you were with my wife when I'm away. Morrisey, take her to my wife when you reach headquarters. And tell Silvano to give you a *good* beef, my compliments." He wheeled his horse, face settling into stern lines. "Right now I'm finding General Bee!" He and his *vaqueros* were off in white dust.

Vin turned to see Jare smiling shyly at Estrella. "Thanks, Miss Estrella. You got us out of a tough spot." She blushed.

"That is well, for you have all helped me." She brought them plates of food. The boys ate while the other men hitched up the wagons. Vin stole several glances at Jare.

"Say, when did you learn Spanish?" he finally asked.

"Oh, after that night we sang with Silvano I wanted to know the language and Roncador's helped me out." After a moment's hesitation, Jare added, "Miss Estrella is teaching me, too. Thee ought to learn, Vin. It's mighty pretty talk."

Once Vin would have snorted. Now, thinking, he said, "Today it was mighty useful. They might have hung us right off if you hadn't been able to palaver some."

Jare, embarrassed or shocked at the praise, ducked his head and ate faster, while Vin continued in his thoughts.

He used to naturally low-rate anything Jare did as sissy or impractical. But his Spanish had come in handy today, and there had been nothing sissy or "Quakerish" about twisting that *cimarrón's* tail. Vin shifted uneasily.

Could it be his ideas of courage and manhood had been sort of narrow and confined to glorious blood-and-thunder demonstrations? Was he, not Jare, the one who didn't look straight at things?

He scoffed the notion aside at once.

NIGHT RAIDERS

The Missouri train reached Santa Gertrudis, the ranch head-quarters, on November 12, several days after Bee foundered in with his breathless escort and rushed supply wagons. He was still camped at the ranch, no doubt wondering how his flight, commanded though it had been, looked to the rest of the world. Mark, after reporting to him, came back to camp, frowning heavily.

"This stuff we hauled from Fort Brown is needed for the border troops. General Bee is routing the salvaged supplies to Laredo and Eagle Pass. I know you all are sick of the border and need to get home. If you want, you can unload and keep going north. But I'm driving to the Rio again, and I hope you will."

"So Bee can burn what we haul?" muttered Roncador.

Mark spoke sharply. "As long as we control part of the border, there's a chance to get cotton across the Rio, into Mexico, and out to the foreign ships. It'll be further, more costly, lots more dangerous, but it's still an artery—and that's important if you're bleeding to death!"

It wasn't one person bleeding. It was the South.

But I want to be a soldier! Pa'd just have to let me after I get home, especially since I stayed with the cotton while Darcy took off. While the other teamsters looked questioningly at each other, Vin stared at the ground.

Who wanted to whomp mules around down here at the edge

of nowhere? The war was a long way off, where Darcy rode with a glint of spurs, where officers waved swords, and flags marched proudly. Vin had stuck with his job till the cotton was sold. Surely now he had a right to join the real fighting. Quakers like Jare, old men like Sully, and those like Mark who'd done their battling, could do the hauling.

Vin cleared his throat, glanced up to say that he was through with Wild Horse Desert, that he was heading home and to the army.

Mark's face, tired, disgusted but determined, throttled Vin's speech as effectively as a fist rammed down his throat. Involuntarily, Vin gazed at Mark's ruined leg, the one that hung shorter than the other and always would. Mark was driving wagons, putting up with fatheaded soldiers and officials, not because he wanted to and not for the money, but because *someone* had to; and he was in the place and time.

"I—I'll go to the border," Vin growled. He dug viciously at the sand with his toe. This one trip. That was all. Then he was getting into uniform. But he couldn't, the way things were, refuse Mark right now. Doggone it! It'd sure be simpler and a lot more fun to be like Darcy, see what you wanted to do as what you just naturally ought.

Jare said, "I'll go."

Sure, Vin thought bitterly. *What have you got to lose?*

"This once," declared Sully feelingly. "But danged if won't slog along with the foot-sojers, old as I be, afore I bring another wagon to this forsaken place!"

There was more than one explosive echo of this, but one by one, all agreed, and Mark laughed, standing, it appeared, a little better on his crippled leg.

"That's the way, boys! You'll get enough dirt in your craws to grind your food long after your teeth fall out." He added seriously, "These supplies won't go to waste. There's a Major Santos Benavides at Ringgold who moves his cavalry fast and smart, keeping the cotton routes from San Antonio open. They call him the Gray Ghost of the Border and he sure sounds like Rip Ford's kind of soldier."

"I hope so," Vin said to Jare under his breath.

They stayed two days at the Santa Gertrudis, resting their badly fagged mules and packing the wagons to capacity. Estrella was living in the house with Mrs. King, a quietly pretty, gentle woman with a streak of iron. The night before the wagons were to leave, eight of them headed for Laredo with cotton, the other two filled with supplies for Ringgold, Silvano brought them the beef promised by Captain King. They invited him to stay for the barbecue, and while the meat was basting over an acrid mesquite fire, Estrella came.

Gone were the poncho and trousers. She wore a blue dress with a velvet tie at the neck and her hair was brushed into calm waves. The men, flabbergasted, behaved as if they'd never seen her before, but her smile was the same and when she took the cover off the basket she carried, the spicy fragrance drew them like bees.

"I brought you honey cakes," she said. "Mrs. King helped me make them. I hear you are to go to the border, and I wanted to thank you again for bringing me here."

"It was a pure pleasure," Mark said. Gallantly, he swung down a box for her to sit on. "Won't you stay and have supper with us this last time?"

"I hoped you would ask me. Mrs. King says it is all right. She is very good to me—she gave me this pretty dress. I shall sew many beautiful things for her and the baby who will come before spring."

"That's fine," Mark said heartily. "Well, boys, this is turning into a real shindy—Silvano and barbecue, Miss Estrella and cake! Let's have fun tonight 'cause it's a long way to the Rio!"

Roncador looked up from swabbing fat over the beef. *"Fi-esta!"* he roared. "Get your fiddle, Jare. Clear your throats, everybody! Let's howl and be happy!"

So they ate, and sang and laughed, and in that last of the evening, Jare played to Silvano's and Estrella's singing of a sad-happy song. Vin wished he understood it, the music of the cruel land with its wind that never stopped blowing, its people the brief color against the dun-hued prairie and glittering, hot sky.

Before light next morning, the wagons were rolling, eight of the Missouri train joining the other cotton-carrying, Laredo-bound wagons. Vin and Roncador, Sully and Mark, drove the two supply wagons bound for Ringgold, while Jare herded their horses and some extra mules. The other Missouri beasts had been thrown in with the cotton train's big herd of spare animals.

This road, far less worn than the one to Brownsville, disappeared at times into barren earth, baked chalk-white and hard, but there was more brush and somewhat better graze. So far they had found water at least once a day. At their night camps, Vin began to learn a little Spanish from Jare's songs, and in the day, when their throats weren't too dry, Roncador taught him.

"Just cowpen Spanish and precious little of that," said the cook. "Guess it's better than nothing, though."

They were five days from the ranch when a lone rider from the southwest rode up to them during the noon stop. Except for a black felt hat with the Lone Star of Texas on it and high jackboots, the man looked like a *vaquero*. Coming to earth in an agile slide, he spoke in good English.

"Corporal Torres of the Thirty-Third Texas Cavalry, courier for Major Santos Benavides. You are the wagons from the Santa Gertrudis bound for Ringgold?"

"That's right," said Mark, puzzled. "Have a cup of coffee? Some dinner?"

The soldier relaxed a bit. "I would relish it, *señor*." But he gave his news before he sat down. "You must proceed to Laredo. My Major has learned that Union troops are coming upriver under E. J. Davis."

"Davis! The Brownsville renegade?"

"Now he is a colonel of cavalry. Our spies downriver say he left Brownsville with a hundred mounted men, a hundred infantry in wagons, and one hundred-fifty cavalry and a howitzer on a steamship. He planned to make thirty miles a day."

Mark whistled. "Some expedition! What's he supposed to do?"

"Clean out Ringgold Barracks—defeat Major Benavides."

"Can he do it?"

The courier grinned, dug hungrily into the plate of food Jare brought him. "He can't catch us. We'll play with him, *señor*, hide-and-seek, back and forth across the Rio. Most of us with the Major are of the Rio Grande. But it is better for wagons and regular troops to be in Laredo. Yankees would have a hard time getting that far, for the steamers cannot run further than Rio Grande City even when the river is high."

"How will we get to Laredo?" pondered Mark.

"I'll show you the way." The corporal put down his cup and plate. "We can start as soon as you are ready."

During the next days as they angled northwest, the corporal told them the incredible story of Santos Benavides. Grandson of the founder of Laredo, Benavides had been fighting Indians or bandits from his boyhood, among them the green-eyed power of Tamaulipas, Cheno Cortina. Like Ford, he had been a Ranger before the war, and now, with about one hundred and twenty loyal Texas-Mexicans he was the Confederacy's last defense along the Rio Grande cotton routes.

Vin got burning angry as the corporal explained how these men were doing their vital work unrecognized and at their own expense. They hadn't been paid in months and their requests for guns and ammunition were mostly ignored.

"Bet your Major feels like chucking it all and fighting where he'll be appreciated," Vin burst out once.

"Appreciated?" The corporal looked up in surprise. "But this is where he is *needed*."

Benavides had a good spy system downriver for the corporal was also able to tell what had been going on in Matamoros while the Union occupied Brownsville. Finally, the Missourians heard the truth out of the wild rumors Bee's informants had circulated.

On November 1, twenty-six Union transports carrying almost seven thousand troops had tried to land, but couldn't because of the storm, though at noon they did manage to plant the Union flag on Brazos Island. It was November 3 before soldiers could begin making their way to the beach, amid capsizing landing boats and weather that pounded four of the big transports to the point of distress. Not a dry round of ammunition made the shore, and the difficult, almost impossible landing dragged on for three days with horses and artillery giving endless trouble.

Several score well-led men could have shoved them back. But Bee had quivered nervously at the fort and left it and the town in flames three days before General Nathaniel Banks marched into Brownsville with his men, and put the demoralized town under martial law commanded by General Dana.

The occupation had been a relief for in the days between Bee's flight and Banks' arrival, looters and scoundrels had ranged the streets, taking what they wanted from stores and houses, shooting down people in their own yards. Fortunately, most of the population had managed to get to Matamoros and many had stayed there, though some citizens and the mayor of Brownsville had taken the oath of allegiance to the Union.

On the day Banks took Brownsville, a Mexican general named Cobos had seized Matamoros and locked up the military governor, Ruiz, with the help of Cheno Cortina. While Cobos was preparing to shoot Ruiz, Cortina arrested Cobos and had his amazed ex-friend shot. Ruiz was frightened out of the city and Cortina took over the rule of northeast Mexico though a puppet governor was installed under his protection.

Cortina, old enemy of Rip Ford, Benavides, and other Confederates, won Banks' favor by turning over to him for Union disposal three steamers belonging to King and Kenedy which had been lightering cotton out to the foreign merchant ships. These steamers were now being used to carry Union supplies—and it was in one of them that Davis' howitzer and troops were coming upriver.

"I remember Banks," said Mark. "Mr. Commissary Banks, we called him in Virginia. He supplied Stonewall Jackson in fine style—lots better than the Confederacy did. In the Valley campaign alone Banks left us a warehouse full of medical stores, over nine thousand small arms, two cannons and plenty of ammunition, all kinds of bacon, sugar, coffee, salt, bread, flour and cheese, a hundred head of cattle and thousands of dollars' worth of quartermaster stuff!" Blissfully enumerating these windfalls, Mark smiled. "And now he's here!"

"No," corrected the corporal. "He left General Dana in charge and went back north. Right now all is cozy between Dana and Cortina. What Dana doesn't know is that Cortina hates all gringos and would play the Union off in a minute if it would benefit Mexico or Cheno."

Early in December they reached Laredo and reported to the fort. Vin hoped for a glimpse of Benavides, but a soldier said the commander was off scouring the road to San Antonio of bandits who had been robbing the cotton trains. Leaving the supplies which had come such a tortuous route from Fort Brown, the Missouri wagons stayed in Laredo a few days while the mules rested. Then, laden with drugs and powder freshly brought in from Mexico, Vin's party took the San Antonio road.

"Be careful," warned Corporal Torres as they left. "We hear that General Dana learned of thousands of bales of cotton moving through here and Eagle Pass and he has said he means to make the routes between the border and San Antonio so dangerous that 'neither Jew nor Gentile' will travel them. He says that what can't be captured should be killed or burned."

Roncador snorted through his warped nostrils. "Big words —if he can back them up."

"He's encouraging irregulars—plain bandits, really—to ambush the wagons," said Torres. A proud grin replaced his concerned expression. "We hear, too, that Dana has tried to find out from the United States consul at Matamoros whether Major Benavides is Mexican or a Confederate, since he is in Mexico a good deal of the time. Dana would like to get the Mexican authorities to catch him. But the Major is a man of the Rio. He knows well the uses of *el otro lado*."

"Good luck to him," said Mark feelingly. "I hope we meet. And thanks, Corporal Torres, for guiding us across that desert."

The corporal smiled, shrugged. "It was nothing. Go with God."

Mark had learned that the other eight Missouri wagons had gone to San Antonio after unloading and Brother Elkanah, put in charge by Mark, had left word that they would wait there for their friends. And of course, San Antonio was that much further north, that much nearer home. Vin's lungs swelled excitedly at the thought of how he would get Pa to let him volunteer. Of course he'd stay home a week or two, help get the spring planting done, and soak up Mama's cooking and gentle voice. But then he'd find Darcy—

That night as they sat around the fire eating, Mark looked around and spoke deliberately. "I don't think I'll go back to Missouri. Brother Elkanah can take charge. I'm going to help move cotton. Probably hire on with King."

"But—" Vin started.

"The wickedest part of the route sounds like it'll be from San Antonio to the border." Mark grinned and flexed his big arms. "I can't anyways march or sit a saddle with the cavalry, but I reckon I can handle mules and bandits!"

So this was going to be Mark's war—hustling cotton, this was the place he was picking to finish his private battle. Admiration and a sympathy that Mark's nature would never accept, welled up in Vin even as he glanced down to avoid his friend's searching gaze.

Couldn't Mark understand? Sure, the cotton was important, and getting it to Mexico was hard and dangerous. But—well, it wasn't the *war,* the one Darcy had already gone to. Mark had done his part of the real fighting. It was credit and honor to him now to take on this thankless, unrecognized chore here at the edge of nowhere. Only it wouldn't be any credit to someone almost seventeen years old, Vin Clayburn, to be exact.

"I'll stay, too," said Jare, having thought it all out, but only the surface of his dark eyes gave back Mark's pleased smile.

Roncador, frowning, didn't speak. Sully, with a sigh, just looked north. He was old and very tired. "I—I guess I'll bring a wagon next summer, God willing," he murmured.

"Not me," Vin promised feelingly. "Back to Missouri! And then to the war!"

Mark stood up. "Seems we all have plans. Still, we have to sleep. We'd better take turns standing watch."

"I'll take it first," Sully offered. His white hair glowed in the firelight like a halo till he looked like a spirit. "I'm awake now, but later on I won't be able to stay that way."

It had been cold all day but the setting of the sun had taken the last hint of friendliness out of the wind which whipped their blankets about their legs and arms as they got ready to bed down.

"Never thought I'd want to sleep by a mule," Mark grumbled, "but I would if one'd get between me and that north wind! Let's get close together. Keep your guns handy. And, hey, Roncky! Try not to snore so loud you bring Indians or bandits from more than five miles around!"

"Hmmf!" seethed Roncador, halting in the act of spreading his blankets north of Mark. "Just for that I'll leave you biting the wind and I'll snug down by Vin."

Vin hunched his elbow under his cheek, burrowing out a depression in the earth, sighed heavily through his whole body, and dropped into sleep as one might fall down a cistern.

Just as sharply, just as clearly, he woke to the sound of a step near his head, a grinding in the sand. Muscles taut, ears humming with tension, he sensed a presence above him, heard the shuffle of feet inside the wagon circle.

Whoever it was, there were more than one. Sully must have dozed or they'd silenced him. Vin felt cold and hot at once, and his heart swelled and throbbed like hoofbeats, though his brain, ticking away as if it had nothing to do with this, told him how to act.

In one second, he kicked back at Roncador, yelling, "Raid!" and dived for the legs that had stopped by his blanket. As he twisted over in the dirt with a wiry bad-smelling body, Vin heard the subdued scuffle of steps change into running, Roncador give a final snortle as he scrambled up, and a stifled cry from Sully.

It was thick dark. Vin caught Mark's startled roar, thought he heard Jare, and then it was a confusion of grunts, shouts, trampling feet and gasping struggles which merged in Vin's ears with the thundering pain of his breath and the hoarse rasping in his opponent's throat as they swayed and sought out each other in the night, grappling for a hold that would disable the other. An elbow dug into Vin's stomach, sledging out his breath, and a bony arm locked under his neck, hauling it backwards.

Red and green lights exploded before Vin. He kicked desperately, thrust with his jackknifed knee into the other's side. The man's hold loosed for the barest second. Vin wrenched free, rolling away. From his knees he launched himself towards the sound of his onrushing enemy, taking him in the stomach with his head. The hard shock snapped Vin's neck smartly but it must have partially stunned its recipient. Vin floundered triumphantly upon him, hunting his throat, as the downed man fought for air.

"Come on, boys!" The voice came from beyond the wagons. "We'll hit 'em when we can see what we're doing! Fade out for now!"

The body under Vin arched, doubled, sent Vin sprawling; as Vin groped to his knees a boot took him in the side of the head. By the time Vin decided he was alive and not split wide open down the skull, the sound of hooves drummed back tauntingly. The attackers were gone.

GRAY GHOST OF THE BORDER

As Vin climbed dizzily to his feet, Mark's voice came softly, "Everyone all right?"

"Yes," said Vin. Jare echoed him, but his words sounded thick as if they came from between cut lips.

"I'd be fine if I knew I'd get to settle with that spawn who stepped on my bunion!" fumed Roncador.

Sully's only answer was a moan, at least they supposed it was his. Bumping into each other in their haste, the other four men ran towards the direction of shallow breathing. "I've got him," Mark said. "Where are you hurt, old-timer?"

"I—" Sully's tone climbed as if at sudden, vivid pain. "My shoulder, Mark. Don't joggle it—"

"I'll be easy as I can. Can't make a light. Could bring those varmints back. They didn't knife you, did they?"

"No, one of 'em just about wrung my arm off, though, before he clipped me on the head." Dread raised the quavering old voice. "Say! You boys, you're none of you hurt?"

"Just roughed up a little," Mark soothed. A smothered groan, then Mark's relieved verdict. "Your shoulder's probably sprained but no bones are broken."

Shame muted Sully's words. "I—must of gone to sleep. We could have all been killed, and it'd have been my fault!"

"Anyone might have dozed," said Mark briskly. "Don't fret about it. We'll tie up your arm so it won't be weight to your shoulder and then we'd better try to rest. I think our

96

sneaky friends will be back from what one hollered, and to try it in daylight, there must be quite a few."

In the blackness, Jare rubbed grease on Sully's shoulder and Roncador put a sling on his arm, made from Vin's extra shirt. Mark stood watch while the others went back to their blankets, Sully bundled in the midst for warmth.

Vin's body ached, from the fight and the usual weariness, but he couldn't sleep right away. The first flush of triumph had been drowned by the realization that they were like rabbits in a snare waiting for the trapper's morning rounds.

Out there in the night the raiders were camped and at the moment they chose they would probably come down on the wagons so fast there'd be little chance to fight. Sully could neither drive nor handle a rifle. Jare wouldn't shoot. That left three men to defend the wagons and try to drive at the same time!

Sweet pickings!

I wish they'd gone ahead and tried to finish us tonight, Vin thought bitterly. The bandits must have spotted them during the day and waited till dark to attack, counting on wiping out the teamsters and enjoying their loot with no risk to themselves. Vin drew what comfort he could from thinking it wouldn't be that easy now. A few bandits, at least, would wish they'd kept riding the other direction . . .

The next thing he knew, Mark was shaking him. "Your watch, lad." As Vin staggered sleepily up, the big hands clasped his shoulders. "You saved our hides with your warning, Vin. Well done!"

A glow of pleasure tingled through Vin even as he wondered, *Saved us for how long?*

He was so jumpy that it was no temptation to drowse. The norther howled so that Vin was sure a whole troop could come down on them close before being heard. Prowling between the wagons, Vin wished it were dawn. He wanted to get moving, meet whatever the day was going to hold. They might be lucky, something could happen; so long as they were alive they had a chance.

This desert had one virtue. An ambush was hard to set up. Flat land and scrubby trees gave small concealment. The bandits would almost have to attack them openly and maybe they'd decide two wagons weren't worth it.

That consoling thought had to be discarded at once, though. Wagons coming from the Rio Grande were pretty sure to carry war supplies, expensive things. And if there were only two wagons, there were only a few men to defend them. Balanced out. Vin ruefully gazed out into the night that hid so many things he wondered about.

Could the raiders be part of General Dana's plan to make the route dangerous? If so, it was some way to run a war! But then—Beauregard Jims, Kraus, Bee, the gutted town of Brownsville, Estrella following the wagons with her sewing machine salvaged from fire—war was a far cry from what Vin had imagined it. He spat out acrid dust and hugged himself against the biting wind.

Well, yes, that was war down here. What could you expect? But where Darcy was there'd be drums and flags, the generals with names like flashing swords. Lee, Shelby, Stonewall Jackson (dead at Chancellorsville, but who could forget him?), Morgan the Raider—*their* fights were the kind Vin meant to get into.

And he would. Just as soon as the wagons were back in Missouri and Pa could spare him from the heavy spring work. In the east, as if blown by the wind, a few reddish streaks appeared, piercing Vin's dreams.

He had to laugh. People were mighty funny. Here he was planning months ahead when this day, without wonderful luck, might be his last. He didn't really believe it—but probably no one ever did. Vin started a fire, robbing some rat ranches of their sticks and dry dung. These were hills made by rats out of earth and refuse. He was grinding the coffee when Roncador cut off the middle of a tremendous snore and sat up. Seeing Vin at work, he blinked and rubbed his eyes.

"I'm still dreamin'! No, I see it now! You're trying to do some good deeds fast-like to ease you by Saint Peter!"

"Some thanks!" retorted Vin. He finished his chore and vacated the cook area, going with Jare and Mark to water the mules in the little creek they were camped by.

The norther had begun to wane with the daylight and by the time breakfast was over and they were ready to move out, the clouds were gone and a summer-bright sun warmed the chill edges of an easterly breeze. Sully, refusing help, scrambled into the wagon by Mark.

"I won't be much help to you otherwise," he lamented, "but I'll sure keep a good lookout!"

"That's what we need," Mark nodded. "Now, boys, if we run into trouble, let's swing the wagons together and take what cover we can between them. We're dealing with sneak-thieves. Maybe they'll have no taste for bullets."

"I've eaten better desserts myself," grinned Roncador.

The only good thing about their waterless nooning was that no bandits appeared. As the afternoon clumped slowly through the miles, Vin began to dare to think the raiders had given them up as too puny a profit for the risk. Jare, perhaps arrived at the same hope, was whistling *Clementine* as he herded their extra animals.

"There's an arroyo ahead," Mark called. "Hope there's some water in it."

The mules' quickened pace made it seem likely. Like horses, they could scent water. Roncador said more than one desert traveler had been saved because his thirsty animals carried him to the water they had somehow known was there.

From the brink of the deep gully, Mark shouted back, "Scummy, but it's wet! We'll cross and make camp on the other side."

It was a steep grade. Following Mark's wagon, Vin pulled back on the team while Roncador worked the brake. As the wagon rattled across baked clay, Vin saw Sully's arm wave, heard his warning cry.

"Bandits!"

From behind a curve of the arroyo wall burst a dozen riders. Their attackers of last night, cunningly picking this one chance for an ambush? Swinging the whip, Vin brought his wagon alongside Mark's. Mark cut his at an angle so the endgates bumped together, leaving a wedge-shape of space.

"Let the mules scatter," Mark called to Jare who was trying to keep his small herd together. "Get between the wagons! Sully, you keep our mules pointed out so we won't get ground to pieces. Have your reins looped around the seat good, Vin, got the brake locked? You and Roncador take that side, I'll shoot from here. Jare, you load for us."

Mark's voice sounded thin, strange. The way Vin felt as he loaded, found a slit between the endgates and fired at the closest raider. Missed. But a second after Mark's rifle barked, there was a scream of pain and a riderless horse galloped up the bank. Roncador fired as Jare pressed a loaded rifle into Vin's hands. They managed to keep up a steady firing that way, though not much of it.

The bandits were circling the wagons, shooting and yelling, going so fast Vin had to aim ahead of his picked man, and still missed. Round and round the raiders swept, bullets striking the wagon beds with resounding plunks or burying softly in the earth or canvas. Two of them were gone. For the first time, Vin was conscious of breathing.

Maybe—just maybe, thanks to the protection of the wagons, they might get through this.

A mule screamed. There was a flailing sound of struggle, Sully's frantic adjurations to the team. Vin, in the flash of a glance, saw a mule kicking in its death convulsions. Another, as if poleaxed, was sinking quietly in its traces. Their team-mates had gone wild, kicking, lunging, dragging the wagon forward in spite of Sully's efforts to control them with the lines. Jare thrust the rifle he was loading into Mark's hands and dived for the lead mule, catching his harness, speaking in a soft, calming tone.

How can he? Vin wondered, even in this moment feeling that bewildering mixture of admiration and bafflement he had for Jare now instead of the old easy contempt for someone he thought a coward. Dropping to his stomach, Vin loaded, took careful aim for what might be his last shot. The bandits, whooping with triumph, were speeding close. Roncador's carbine took one but the nine others came on. Vin recognized the raw-boned, yellow-eyed man of the outside just as Mark breathed in outrage, "Trig Medders! Turned renegade!"

Vin started to squeeze the trigger. The raider he was aiming at dropped like a stone, and so did another, though Mark hadn't fired, either. The bandits were checking, pulling their mounts around. They were gone in a clatter over the baked mud, spurring up the arroyo bank. Vin turned to see what they were running from in time to blink as a torrent of hooves sliced past, wild manes and tails carried along by spring-muscled legs. Crouched low to their horses were a stream of riders, some in sombreros, some in black hats with the flashing Texas lone star.

They surged up the grade and disappeared after the thieves. Vin crawled to his knees, dusted off his hands and face. Numb with relief, he stared after the smoky trail of dust.

"Wonder who took Trig and his pals off us?" he croaked.

"Maybe Texas Rangers or an escort for some wagon train," Mark speculated. The big man looked around.

Jare and Sully had got the mules stopped but they were still fractious and on the edge of panic. Sully was white-lipped, sweating; he must have been about to faint with pain from his sprained shoulder. Jare bled from what seemed a grazed scalp.

"I'm fine," he insisted, evading Roncador's worried fingers. "Let's get these dead mules out of the harness before the rest go crazy."

"You sit down," Mark told Sully with rough kindness. "I saw you usin' your teeth and hurt arm and everything but your toenails!"

They soon had the downed mules free of the traces and moved the wagons to the ford. The fight seemed to have lasted hours but it couldn't have taken more than twenty minutes for the sun had barely dipped a fraction further west.

"I don't hear any more firing," Vin said, watching the south bank.

"Probably all over," Mark judged. "Whoever it was after those bandits meant business. Start supper, Roncador. Make plenty of coffee. I imagine our friends will be back."

Excited though they were, Vin and Jare helped Mark water the teams. Their extra animals had only run into a narrowing of the arroyo some distance from the ford where grass grew on banked-up silt with comparative lushness. Jare and Vin strung ropes from a mesquite on one side of the arroyo wall to a scrub willow opposite and left all the stock to graze in this natural corral. Vin was cleaning the caked blood off Jare's creased scalp when Roncador's voice boomed an alert.

"Dust raisin'. Here they come!"

Brushing away Vin's ministrations, Jare got up and watched southwards. Out of the whirl of dust, first on the edge of the bank, then plunging down it, came horsemen. They halted behind their leader who pulled up his lathered horse beside the wagons. Aside from the black hats and a scattering of jack boots, the men were in *vaquero* garb, except for the commander who wore, pridefully, a gray officer's coat. As he swept off his hat, he inclined his dark head, controlling his nervous horse with one strong hand.

"Gentlemen, I am Major Santos Benavides of the Thirty-Third Texas Cavalry." A smile handsomed his lean face. "As you see, we are striving to keep the route open between San Antonio and the border."

Mark offered his hand. "Major, we're beholden. In a few more minutes— Did you catch the thieves?"

"All but one." Benavides made a significant hanging motion. "While we were busy with the others, a gringo escaped into the brush. But he was without a horse and will not last long."

Trig? Vin shivered. It was a bad ending, even for a traitor. Mark shook his head. "He must have been a man who deserted our train near Brownsville. They hit us last night but scooted when they found they couldn't just kill us in the dark."

"Dark or light, they'll kill no more." A rumbling came from the north. The Major nodded towards it. "Twenty wagons we're escorting. Loaded with Louisiana cotton and routed

through the King Ranch. Our scout heard shooting so we
came to investigate." He scanned their party, taking in Sully's
useless arm, Mark's leg.

One old, wounded man, a cripple, two boys, and fat Roncador—Vin guessed they didn't look like much. But he wanted
to shout, *We've come a long hard way, we managed what we
started, to sell our cotton. And we didn't dump or burn our
load when Bee and his Army were running fast!*

"I wish I could detail some men to ride guard for you," the
Major said. "Unfortunately—"

Mark grinned. "Don't apologize. This is war. Those twenty
wagons are worth a lot more than our two." Relief sounded in
Benavides' tone.

"Thousand thanks for understanding." He looked again at
Sully's arm. "I can loan you a driver, though. He knows this
road well and the water places." Turning, the leader pitched
his voice higher and called, "Paco!"

A slender boy not much older than Vin rode forward, gaze
fixed in eager worship on the Major. "You will hitch your
mount to one of the wagons," directed Benavides, seeming to
not observe how the boy's face darkened. "I know you are
a good driver so you will help these people get to San Antonio."

"But, my Major—" began the young soldier in stormy
protest.

Benavides appeared not to hear. "In San Antonio you will
report to Colonel Ford. He may have new information for us.
Then rejoin this command. It is understood?"

Eyes sullen, Paco seemed to be gritting his teeth, but when
he saluted his voice was under control. "It is understood, my
Major."

Slowly, he dismounted. Vin felt sorry for him; he knew how it felt to be nudged out of the exciting, important things and set to dull, if necessary, work. Benavides turned back to Mark.

"The train will camp across the arroyo tonight so at least for the night there should be no trouble."

Roncador grunted approvingly. "Then for the night we'll sleep sound—and it's good to know we'll wake up alive!"

Laughing, Benavides signaled his men. They rode across the stream towards the creaking sound of the wagons. Paco was unsaddling and rubbing his horse, seeming to take care not to look at his new companions. With a shrug, Vin gave up the idea of going over to make friends. Paco's nose was out of joint right now; when he got ready to talk, there'd be time enough. Vin tingled with envy as he watched the slender young man move up to Mark and speak softly.

Mark looked startled. Then he nodded and smiled, made as if to drop a hand on Paco's shoulder. But Paco evaded it without seeming to have noticed the gesture, walked off with a clinking of long-roweled spurs.

At supper, Vin saw Paco wasn't there. His horse was gone, too. "Our guide quit us?" he asked. Mark waved his pipe at the fire across the arroyo.

"He asked to eat and sleep with his friends tonight. Said he'd be here before daylight."

"Mmm," mused Roncador. "Don't think the kid is too pleased to get sent with us. He's got used to fire-eatin' with that Major."

"The Major's some different from Bee," Sully reflected. "I'd like to hear what he says to Bee—or more likely, doesn't say, but thinks!"

After a long pull on his pipe, Mark spoke forgivingly. "Bee belongs at headquarters or a place he understands. This border takes a border man, I can see that."

"General Lee did fine down here." Jare surprised them all by speaking. "That was during the Cortina wars. Estrella says that Rip Ford thought Lee was wonderful even though Lee believed in the rules and Ford, as a borderer, knew thee had to make new ones for the Rio." Spots of color burned in Jare's cheeks and the fiddle lay quiet in his hands. "That was when Ford crossed into Mexico and chased Cortina till he melted away for the hills."

Vin stared at Jare. First Jare learned Spanish and then history! With never a hint to anyone. "Why, Jare, I didn't know you took any stock in soldiers!" Vin blurted.

"I think General Lee is a gentleman." Was there a tinge of hurt in Jare's voice? "He's a kind person, and brave." Abruptly, Jare rose. He got some grease and began to rub Sully's shoulder. Vin, cheeks blazing, wondered why Jare had to be so hard to talk to, so downright impossible to understand. He and this Paco promised to make a pair! And in addition to his other troubles, he, Vin, had to get along with them!

PACO'S PROMISE

They moved out next morning with Paco in Sully's seat by Mark while Sully rode one of the horses. The cotton wagons Benavides was escorting were hitched up and ready to roll as the Missourians passed. Mark pulled up beside the Major, thanked him again and wished him luck.

"The same to you," said Benavides. "And in case young Paco forgets, remind him to report to Colonel Ford."

"You know I will not forget, my Major!" cried Paco. It seemed for a moment his eyes would actually fill with tears.

Benavides' gaze rested on him with measuring affection. "Not even if you see a pretty girl? Or if there is a cockfight?"

From the way Paco bit his lip and fell silent, Benavides referred to past derelictions. *"Ay,* well then, *muchacho!"* laughed the Major. "Drive the mules skilfully and come to me as quickly as may be." He gave a courtly nod to Mark and the others. *"Adiós, señores."*

As Mark's wagon swung into the lead, Vin saw how Paco's mouth drew down beneath the young hawk nose. He either coudn't or wouldn't disguise his feeling at being transformed from one of the Gray Ghost's men to a wagon teamster.

At the noon stop he lay on his back by a wagon, aimlessly jingling his spurs and smoking shuck cigarettes he rolled with deft slim fingers.

"Better fill your plate again," Mark invited. "It'll keep your ribs from rubbing your backbone along about sunset."

Paco sat up like an explosion. "My stomach is already full," he said. "Full of mule's dust! How can anyone endure this turtle pace?"

"You can't gallop with ten thousand pounds of freight," Mark pointed out. His tone was good-humored but he walked off without giving Paco a chance to argue.

Vin was burning. When Paco curled his aristocratic nostrils and snorted, Vin could no longer rein in his tongue. "These wagons aren't any fun but they're important! Doesn't your Major spend his time guarding them?"

"A shepherd guards sheep, too," sniffed Paco. "That does not make them the less smelly or stupid."

"Say!" Vin jumped to his feet as if flicked by the popper of a whip. "You callin' us stupid? You don't smell so good yourself!"

Paco smiled. He blew an infuriating spiral of smoke. "Why, *amigo*, I spoke of sheep!"

Vin continued to smolder even after they were traveling again. Benavides could have this young rooster back right now for all of him! All stuck up because he was a soldier—

And you're mad because you're not. Vin couldn't dodge that truth so he shooed his team along and tried to forget Paco was in the wagon ahead. That night they camped by an almost dry water hole, and the next nooning was completely dry. The graze was so poor that they grained the animals though the poor brutes had a hard time swallowing the dry sustenance.

"Can we hit water by night?" Mark asked Paco who had continued to speak only when he was spoken to and then in such a way that no one tried to talk to him much.

"Maybe six miles," Paco shrugged. "We move so slowly it is hard for me to guess."

"We'll try for it," Mark decided. "Rather push the mules to water than make them do without."

After a two-hour stop instead of the usual four, the teamsters began harnessing the unwilling mules, who, far from understanding it was in order that they might drink that night, exhibited all the meanness possible to mules—which was plenty.

Kicking, biting, sullen, refusing to budge. Vin, rousting one moth-eaten, gray crowbait into its place, heard a highly-seasoned torrent of Spanish along with whacking, meaty sounds. Whirling, Vin saw Paco bring down, again, the butt of his carbine on the head of a mule he was trying to force into line.

"Hey!" shouted Vin.

But Jare, closer to Paco, had already grabbed his arms, spinning the young soldier around.

"Thee must stop that!"

"Must?" Eyes blazing in his narrow face, Paco pulled free easily from the younger boy. "Touch me again, gringo, and I'll use the butt on you!"

Paco whirled back to the mule. Vin, paralyzed by the shock of seeing Jare almost fighting, stumbled over the wagon tongue as he tried to get to Paco before the carbine could descend on the animal.

He was too late. The butt swung down, and it struck, not the mule, but Jare as he dodged in front of the beast. Though the glancing blow landed on Jare's hip, staggering him backwards, he spoke in a quiet voice.

"Thee must not do this."

Paco stared at Jare a minute, pale with rage and disbelief. With a hissing intake of breath, he brought the carbine behind his head, started to swing. Mark, who had been fixing

Sully's arm sling, shouted and started up, but he was too far away. Vin, scrambling over the wagon tongue, launched himself on Paco in a flying spring, gripping him around the knees. Paco grunted.

They went to the ground already wrestling, grappling for advantage. Vin, a little the heavier, caught a breath and found himself perched on top. Paco kicked up. Fiery pain shot down Vin's thigh. He forgot everything but hurting back. He got a handful of Paco's curly black hair, banged his head hard against the packed earth.

"—put some sense into you!" he panted.

But a hand was on his own collar, dragging him back. "Thee," said Jare, "must not do that."

Vin felt his eyes start from his head. "Why, you crazy galoot!" he choked. But he got up, mostly because Mark had hold of him now, too. "You just goin' to stand there and let him beat you to death?"

"All of you simmer down," Mark commanded. He turned to Paco who was dusting himself off furiously as he rose. "Look, young fella, we don't mistreat even mules, no matter how pesky. If you can't remember that, better catch up with Major Benavides."

Paco's contorted face showed he would love to do just that. His hands clenched and unclenched. Finally, swallowing, he stood erect.

"My Major told me to stay with you into San Antonio. That I must do then. But do not blame me if your teams never get harnessed. When I freighted for the army out of San Antonio, the teamsters, even the gringos, knew a mule knows only what is lashed into him." Looking slowly around to Jare, Paco's eyes contracted.

"You I do not comprehend. I do not at all! You will not fight for your own body yet you make a shield for a mule!"

"And kept me from giving you what you had coming," Vin muttered. Paco glared at him but before any more could be said, Mark spoke firmly.

"Forget it! Finish harnessing and let's move out." But he, too, gave Jare a puzzled glance as he moved back to work.

Paco's scornful estimate had been right. They traveled till sundown, but they did reach water, a creek running shallow between crumbled banks that showed its usual level. They unharnessed and camped in silence, too weary for banter even if the nooning's violence hadn't left a sourness in the air. But Vin had been smoldering all afternoon, and after supper, while Jare was poulticing the fetlock of his horse who had gotten a thorn in it, Vin went over to him.

"Get the thorn out?" Vin asked, tongue-tied over his real topic.

"It worked out in the poultice I put on last night," said Jare gladsomely. "Roncador said the pulped inside of a prickly pear would turn the trick, and it did. But there's still a lot of swelling."

Securing the bandage, Jare started back to the campfire. *He* wasn't going to mention that run-in with Paco, Vin saw— but doggone it!

"Jare! Now listen." As Jare paused questioningly, Vin felt a wild, almost angry urge to shake him, try somehow to get through to that maddening contrariwise mind. Using all his self-control, he took a deep breath and let it out in what he thought were careful, reasonable words. "You can't stand in front of someone while they slam you with a carbine. If you won't fight don't get into places where you'll have to. It'll get you killed!"

Amiably, Jare said, "I don't think Paco would hit me more than once again."

"Of all the crazy—!"

Jare grinned. "No, think about it! Thee hit me, I hit thee back, thee hit me, and so it goes. But if I don't hit back, what happens?"

"I think you've lost your mind!"

"Yes, but thee do *think,* not hit. And it's lots harder to hit me if thee do go on with it." A chuckle crept into Jare's voice. "Thee couldn't hit me twice, could thee?"

Vin grunted. "I couldn't, maybe. Some folks would enjoy it."

"Then there'd be something wrong with them."

"Them—or you?" Vin asked with a despairing whistle.

Only it did make a sort of addled, inhuman sense. More woman, or preacher thinking than a man's. Be fine if everyone was like that but till they were— Then who was going to start it?

Not me! Vin thought. He squirmed at the notion. Have folks think him a coward? That would be the worst, not just getting hurt.

But if you believed that was what you should do—and did it—then weren't you really brave? Braver than if you fought because it came naturally when you were mad, and because people would look down on you if you didn't?

Is Jare braver than I am?

Six months ago Vin would have hooted at the question. Now he frowned, defending himself with the haste of a swimmer whose clothes have been stolen and who hears girls coming.

No! Jare's—just different.

Whatever it was that was forcing Vin to look past the outside action to the inner cause—a new and painful experiment—wouldn't let him close it off with that.

Who stayed cool and parleyed when King's vaqueros were ready to stretch your necks? Who volunteered to keep with this dirty work which is dangerous without any glory? Who got in front of Paco's carbine?

All right! Vin surrendered, stumping back to the fire and his blankets. *Jare's braver—and he's welcome to it. I can't act that way! I don't want to.*

It turned bitter cold next day and there was no water either at noon or night. The poor mules had such a brutal time with their dry grain that it hurt to watch them. Mark kicked disgustedly into a clump of prickly pear.

"If there was just some moisture in this stuff since there's no grass! I don't see how cattle live in this country when they can't damp their mouths for miles on end."

Paco, who had wrapped a blanket of silence around himself since the trouble, looked up. He seemed to be debating inwardly. After a moment he spoke in a condescending tone.

"I will teach you a thing."

Show-off spurs jingling, he lit a bundle of mesquite limbs at the fire, crossed to a growth of cactus, and played flame over it, singeing thousands of the fine spines from broad, pulpy leaves. He offered the result to his horse who began to chew it with the fatalism of hunger, thirst, and long practice.

"We do this for our stock when graze is bad," Paco explained. "There's water in the leaves. When it is droughty, horses and cattle often eat the cactus in spite of the needles. Their tongues swell terribly but it lets them live till rain."

"Praise be!" Mark breathed.

The Missourians, even Sully with his good arm, set to burning spines from the dull green pads. After considerable lipping, the mules went to chewing this strange fare. Green pulp dripped comically from their chins. Paco, who had fixed enough for his horse and then settled back to watch, was enjoying this proof of his knowledge and the gringos' ignorance. So much that he smiled and made an actually good-humored remark.

"I have chewed those pads, too, when I was thirsty enough."

Jare said with sincere warmth, "It's lucky thee knew this."

Paco shrugged. After a sharp glance at Jare which detected only plain admiration, Paco said off-handedly, "It is only that I am of the country." But after the mules and horses were supplied, supper was over, and Jare got out the fiddle, Paco, for the first time, didn't prowl off solitarily. He sat by a wagon and seemed to reach for the words of the Missouri songs Jare played first.

When Jare bowed into one of the songs Estrella Riley had taught him, Paco started with pleasure and leaned forward. Almost as if unconsciously, he began to sing, softly at first, then with his head thrown back, sound welling wild and thrilling sad from his throat.

"You are better than the *mariachis,* the professional singers," he told Jare when it was time to sleep and Darcy's fiddle was resting. "I did not know you played—that you had music."

"All men have music." Jare told the fiddle good-night with a last loving sweep of the bow. "Sometimes they just do not listen to it or let it come out."

As he watched Jare, Paco's expression changed from wariness to confusion. From then on he behaved towards Jare with protective respect. But to the other Missourians, he was the same; ignoring Sully and Roncador, obeying Mark, but with

small enthusiasm, giving Vin the rough edge of his super-
cilious smile.

After a few days, it was too much for Vin. "What's eating
you?" he demanded one evening as they were watering the
mules. "Still mad about that tussle?"

"You think something is wrong because I do not give you
the *abrazo*—the embrace of friendship?" Paco asked scath-
ingly.

Vin felt blood heating his face. "Now listen here! I don't
care if you want to pack a grudge. But how come you're all
buddied up to Jare? Why aren't you sore at him, too?"

"He plays most beautifully," said Paco. "Also, in spite of
his strange customs, he is *muy caballero.*"

That was one of the phrases Vin had learned from Jare.
"Oh!" He choked a minute before he could trust himself to
speak. "Jare's a knightly gentleman, is he? While I'm just
an ordinary— What would you say? *Peón?*"

"You are like me." Paco turned full on him. "That is why
we shall have our fight one day!"

"What?"

Paco's slim strong fingers curled into his palms. His chest
heaved. "You rolled me in the dirt, pulled at me with your
dirty stinking hands! You filled my mouth with dust! Our day
will come, gringo, it will come!"

Vin gave a long whistle. "Boy howdy! Full of poison as a
rattlesnake! You left some scars on me, too, remember!"

"That is not honorable, the way it was. Next time we will
fight with dignity. Not with fists like brawling gringos but
with knives!" Paco looked positively happy at the thought.

"Whoa! I don't use a knife."

"Then you'd better learn."

Vin mulled all this over silently for a minute. He couldn't

believe Paco was serious—till he looked at him. "And when are we going to have all this dignified fighting?"

"It will have to wait," Paco said, in a sad voice. "My Major would not want it. But the war will not last forever, we will not always be on the same side! Then—" And Paco's eyes glittered like a blade unsheathed. In spite of himself, Vin felt an icy, thin chill tickle up his spine.

"If you have anything to settle, better do it now," he counseled, managing what he hoped was a careless laugh. "I'm heading back to Missouri and from there to the big war. You'll sure never see me scratching through this desert again!"

Paco smoothed, beneath his shirt, the knife he carried in a scabbard slung from his neck. "Have no concern. I will find you."

"Any time," Vin said, turning back to the animals. He had never been in an argument that couldn't be ended with wrestling or fists, but it seemed this quarrel with Paco was a horse of another color.

Not that Vin was afraid, exactly. It was just worrisome to have someone treasuring up hatred to use in a duel after the war was over. *Shucks,* Vin told himself, I won't be here. *And if he wants to come to Missouri for a fight I reckon I can oblige him!*

It was Christmas Eve when they rumbled into San Antonio. From some distance Vin had seen a huge fortress-like place which Roncador explained was a mission built by Indians under the direction of Spanish missionaries. Farms were laid out along the river, and irrigation canals threaded both these and the city. Huts like those seen on the border, made of mesquite limbs daubed with clay and thatched with prairie grass, squatted against more prosperous homes of sun-dried brick, while around the main *plazas* or town squares were solid lines of stone houses with flat roofs.

As they rattled through the crowded streets, Vin stared eagerly about. He would have known it was holiday time even if he'd lost track of the date, for the people had the gaiety that is the same anywhere when the usual order of things is bundled away. And were there ever such people!

Sunburned men in leather shirts and leggings and Indian moccasins; men in broad-brimmed hats with silver ornaments or beads, calico shirts and gay sashes; soldiers, regular and irregular, in every conceivable combination of military and civilian attire; sober-suited businessmen; *vaqueros* disdaining to walk; and women, who except for a few Anglos, wore black shawls about their heads and shoulders.

Over there—the ruined building with the tumbled walls— Roncador dug Vin in the ribs, and pointed. "The Alamo, boy! Take a good look. I was through here a few years after Santa Ana took it and saw where the ashes of Bowie, Travis and the others are buried over under some peach trees. About a hundred and eighty men took care of over a thousand Mexicans. Not sure how many, exactly, because there were too many to bury in the mission graveyard and the rest were thrown in the San Antonio River."

Vin, like everyone else, had heard of the Alamo. He stared at the still beautiful scrollwork on the front wall, the doorway with a crown and shield above it.

"I've heard," muttered Roncador, "that after the first Mexican attack when the Texans picked off so many, the Mexican bands were told to play the *Degüello*. The name of the song means throat-cutting. When it's played during battle, it means no quarter for the enemy, no surrenders."

How had it felt inside the mission, looking out at an army of thousands camped across the river, knowing it was the end, that there could be no help; that the end was sure? Vin chilled at the thought, but mixed with the horror and sadness was pride. The doomed hadn't known or guessed their fight would become a battle cry that would spur others on to victory over Santa Ana the very next month and independence for Texas.

Hadn't it seemed to the trapped fighters that they were deserted, left to play out a forlorn game? Had they felt like heroes or bone-tired men; some, sick like Bowie, fighting from the bottom of physical wretchedness to fulfill their own notion of honor, since no one else would see or care? Vin realized suddenly that even when death is the certain result, it is harder to act well without an audience than when one knows one is being watched and judged.

"Watch out where you're goin'," Roncador warned. Vin blinked hastily and swallowed.

"You know," he said, thinking out loud, "I just now see what a text that Brother Elkanah preached once means. It didn't make any sense then, about he that loseth his life shall find it. These men would have died sometime anyway, been forgotten. Now we'll remember them."

And he was glad, oh, so glad, that he would be free soon to join the army, show he could be brave, too.

NEW RECRUIT

It was sundown by the time they reported in at the fort and got permission to corral their mules. Brother Elkanah and the other Missourians had already got there, but most of them were in town watching the celebrations. Vin and Jare were going to the wagons after tending the animals when Paco rode up. He had the *vaquero's* dread of walking and had saddled his horse in order to ride the short distance to the headquarters.

"I am to report back to Colonel Ford before I leave tomorrow," he said. "I have permission to spend the night at my aunt's." The next remarks were directed pointedly to Jare. "Will you not come with me? *Tía* would be very glad. Later we could watch *Las Posadas*. That is sort of a Christmas play and you would like it."

"Why, thanks," said Jare delightedly. "I'll—" His gaze moved to Vin who knelt to pull a nonexistent burr out of his pants. "Thanks anyway," Jare decided, "but I'd better stay here."

"No need for that," Vin growled.

"Why, Vin must come, too," Paco added smooth as cream and as if he had meant so all along. "*Tía* will have cakes and cookies and thick chocolate. And she has little company. This will be pleasure for her."

Jare looked pleadingly at Vin. It was plain he wanted to go. For himself, Vin would have refused, but Jare's loyalty put him on the spot. Besides he, too, wanted to see the town and people; his mouth watered at the mention of cookies and chocolate after months of beans.

"Let's go," he said.

Paco reluctantly consented to walk so his companions could see more. They passed homes whose thick walls presented a solid front to the street except for grilled gates which showed inner gardens and shade trees. After about an hour's stroll, the boys stopped at one of these grilled gate entrances. Paco put his fingers in his mouth and gave an odd fluting whistle. While they waited, Vin looked around.

This was certainly a good way to keep private though living close to people. In Missouri towns the yards and gardens mostly lay exposed to the public eye, and neighbors would have been mad if anyone had walled in their place like this. He wished his mother could see it.

"I wouldn't live in town," she had said once, scornfully. "Gossips watching your clothesline to see how often you change your sheets and if your clothes need mending!"

Vin had learned not to think often of home, but now a painful lump swelled in his throat. It'd be lonesome for his folks this holiday with both sons gone. He hoped they'd be visiting or having company. And Darcy—where was he? What kind of Christmases did soldiers have?

Through the elaborate grillwork of the gate peered a brown monkey face. The suspicion on it glowed into joy.

"Paquito! *Ay, la madama*—" and much more in Spanish, as metal clicked, and the heavy gate swung open.

Paco and the old man embraced, patting each other on the back. While questions flew back and forth in Spanish, Vin looked around. The tiny garden hardly seemed to justify a wall, but even in the dark it gave a sense of restfulness, and birds twittered at being roused. An arched walkway ran the length of the house and from one of these openings bustled a plump small woman. The wizened gatekeeper disappeared through an arch like a gnome or elf in some story while the lady caught Paco in her arms, rocking him. He squirmed embarrassedly, towering above her, as she crooned.

"Paco. Paquito *mío!*"

Though he couldn't understand the rest of what she said, Vin reckoned it was about what his several aunts would tell him if, after an absence, he turned up unexpectedly, except for Aunt Sara. She had never married and her greetings consisted of calling him "Vincent" and bestowing a kiss on his cheek that felt like a hen's peck. This aunt of Paco's was the right kind, though; she smelled of spices and good cooking, and her laughter was deep and natural in the way of people who do it as easily as they breathe. It took a while, but Paco managed to disengage himself and introduce Jare and Vin.

Taking their hands, she welcomed them with a sincerity that a different language couldn't hide. Vin just bowed, but Jare replied in words that must have made up in content for anything they lacked in grammar, for her laughter flowed delightedly as she shooed them into her kitchen.

And what a kitchen! After days and weeks and months of camp fare, this room smelled like heaven. Vin's stomach rumbled ferociously while he struggled to keep from audibly sniffing in the delicious odor of cinnamon, baking cookies, and other things he couldn't identify.

Tía Luisa settled them on a carved heavy bench before a wood table worn smooth and white with scouring. She brought mugs of creamy milk, and a basket of cookies and small decorated cakes, issuing directions to the old woman who was tending the oven and was evidently a servant, perhaps the wife of the gatekeeper. This woman brought baked squash and chicken with rice, obviously left from supper for it was still warm. She chatted while they ate, and between pauses in the talk, Jare caught Vin up on what was being said.

"The Christmas celebrations have been handsome this year in spite of the war. Plays and processions have been going on for over a week. Doña Luisa wishes that Paco's mother and family, who live in Eagle Pass, were here to see everything and to visit."

Doña Luisa smiled on the two Missouri boys, said something and laughed. "She says," translated Jare with a grin, "that you have pretty eyes. They are like those of a Frenchman's she wished to marry long ago." Paco chortled.

Pretty eyes! Vin felt his face heating up, and he took refuge behind his milk till Doña Luisa switched her attention back to Paco.

"She says we'd better hurry if we want to see *Las Posadas*," explained Jare. They finished eating and then, hands full of fragrant cakes Doña Luisa had pressed on them, passed into the street to fall in quickly with a procession led by a man in a long cloak and carrying a staff, and a woman, heavily muffled, upon a mule.

"No getting away from those long-eared critters even in town," Vin whispered, but Jare, eyes fixed intently on the man and woman who had stopped before a house, didn't seem to hear.

The man knocked at the door. From inside came a challenge which the man portraying Joseph answered in a sort of chant which Jare, with a start at Vin's sharp nudge, translated.

> Sir, I beg you of your charity
> To give shelter to this lady.

Jare imitated the gruff voice in the answer.

My inn is for those with silver.
God help him who has none.

The story had never seemed so real as it did now, following the woman who seemed ready to fall from the mule in weariness. From door to door she went, being always refused, till Vin wondered if this would go on all night. He was about to say that interesting as this was he had to get some sleep, when a door finally opened to Joseph's knock, disclosing a long, warmly lit room.

At the far end was a sort of altar with a figure of the Christ Child in the manger. Around it were men brilliantly garbed as shepherds and wise men. Bells rang and from the street came noisy explosions of fireworks.

"Now," said Paco, eyes softened and proud, "the *padre* will hold Mass. Do you not like it, this celebration of my people?"

Later, as Vin stretched out beside Jare on a shuck mattress at Doña Luisa's, it seemed a bright, high-colored dream from another world, one he'd remember all about and tell Mother. He was glad there'd be one happily exciting thing to tell her before he gave his decision to go fight. He decided in a sleepy glow of well-being that Paco wasn't so bad. They might even have made friends had chance kept them together longer.

Next morning, after early breakfast, the boys warmly told Doña Luisa good-by and went back to the Post. Telling Mark that Colonel Ford wanted to see him, Paco saddled. Restored to his old glory, he rode up beside Vin and Jare.

"*Vaya con Dios,*" he said to Jare. "I hope, truly, we meet again." He bent, then, a dark insolent stare on Vin, more startling because they had just walked together in peace, laughed over shared food at Doña Luisa's.

"We *will* meet," the young soldier promised. "The more surely since you prefer to whip mules than *Yanquis.*" Back very straight, he wheeled and rode towards headquarters to make his final report.

Stricken, trembling with fury, Vin took one long stride after the horseman, choked on the dust, and tried to wrest free of Jare's hand.

"That two-faced—! I'll show him!"

"He will not fight thee now," Jare reminded. "He is vowed to his Major and determined to keep out of trouble."

"He's going about it in a funny way," Vin said. "How about that? Still sore because I hit him!"

Jare's brows met in a troubled frown. "That was my fault."

That had been Vin's private thought, too, but he shrugged it off, managed to laugh though the taunt stung him like a poison rash. "You're not to blame, Jare. I'd whomp him again if I had the chance." To prevent the sermon Jare seemed ready to preach, Vin turned away. "Don't worry. He wants to wait till after the war for our great big duel and I doubt I'll ever see him again."

An hour later, with a fresh-shaven, clean-shirted Mark in the lead, some of the Missourians went to headquarters. Vin hoped they'd get to see Colonel Ford—and that the famous border-fighter would speak to him even though he might wonder why Vin wasn't in the army.

But the Colonel wasn't around headquarters. Looking up from a batch of papers, a sergeant grinned and advised,

"Take a look in the infirmary. Colonel Ford just cain't forget he set out to be a doctor."

As soon as Vin saw the dismal place, he was sure no one would report there till in extremity. Fitful coughing rose over the heavy breathing of several men who lay asleep. A graying, bearded officer turned from fixing a fresh bandage about the head of a patient and spoke sharply to the attendant hovering nervously by the bed.

"That dressing hadn't been changed in days. Now keep it clean, understand?"

"But, sir," whined the man, "there's only me to see to everything!"

"If you don't start seeing better, I'll see if you can't go to the hot war and improve your eyesight." Noticing the Missourians, the officer gave his patient a few quiet words and a reassuring press on the shoulder before he strode towards the group at the door.

"Gentlemen, would one of you be Mr. Morrisey?"

Mark put out his hand. "I am. And you're Colonel Ford?" From the way they exchanged glances and shook hands, they liked each other.

"I'd like to send a message by you to Captain King," Ford said. His straight mouth quirked humorously. "From what young Paco says, you'd get it there." Mark laughed but his tone was rueful.

"If that boy had anything good to say of me, I'm astonished to death."

Smiling, Ford led the way outside. "Paco's a hothead but he has good instincts. He told me you carried your full load to Santa Gertrudis and then volunteered for the haul south. He respects you for that whether he let on that he did or not. Let's go to my quarters and talk."

Brother Elkanah and the other teamsters decided to look around the Post but Mark asked if Vin and Jare could come with him. "Certainly," Ford said. Vin squirmed as the soldier's keen glance raked him, wishing he could cry out that as soon as he got back to Missouri he was going to the war.

Inside a Spartan room, Ford let his visitors sit on the bed while he sat by a table spread with maps and military histories. How it must have galled this man to hold down the ignominious chore of conscripting men while Magruder and Bee lost the strategic border Ford understood so well and had shrewdly defended.

"I'm getting back in the field," he said. His grave voice had an underlying thrill of gladness. "While I try to recruit men, I'm collecting supplies for a three-month expedition. King can furnish them, I hope." Vin could almost feel his ears pick up. Recruiting . . . ?

"You getting many volunteers?" Mark asked with the interest of an old soldier.

"Some kids and older men, quite a bunch of my old Rangers." Ford sighed. "The prime soldiers are already siphoned off to the east, of course. I've got a tough job on my hands and not much to do it with."

But you'll do your best. Blood pounded fast and hard in Vin's ears.

Before he quite knew what he was doing, he blurted, "I'll join you, Colonel." He was on his feet, and blood pumped quick and hot through him though he could see everything sharp and clear, suddenly, as if it had just rained. He was even aware of the startled faces of Mark and Jare.

Almost at once he was sorry, wished he'd at least thought it over. The big war, the one with Darcy, that was what he'd intended—

"How old are you, lad?" asked Ford.

"Seventeen in April, sir. I'm healthy and—"

Ford chuckled. The look in his deep eyes and new spirit in his voice made Vin a little happier about his rash act. Even if he served in a ragtag little war, he was fighting under a big man. "I won't study your teeth like a horse trader, son. I'm pleased to have you. And since you're not assigned to anything yet, I'll let you carry my message to the King Ranch. Get your things and report back to me here."

Vin, with a shock, remembered the train, the return trip to Missouri. He'd been so fired-up, he'd forgotten everything but getting into some action. He turned to Mark.

"I— Oh, shucks, Mark! Is there any way for the wagon and money to go home without me?"

Mark studied over it long enough so that Vin knew his answer was accurate when it came. "Well, son, with me stayin' at the King with my wagons, there'll be a few spare teamsters takin' the Missouri trail. I'll bet Sully would drive your wagon, and Brother Elkanah can take your money safe. But if you're bound on this, you better write your folks and explain."

That would be kind of a hard letter to write. Mother would cry and Pa was liable to be angry, especially after Darcy. As if his parents could hear, Vin looked at Mark. "I was joining up as soon as I got home anyhow. You do know how I feel, don't you, Mark?"

Mark's eyes blazed green a moment; then a smile eased the grim lines in his face. "I understand, lad. If you feel like this is your time and place, I won't hinder you."

"Good!" said Ford. "As soon as you come back from the King Ranch, I'll induct you neat and final." His smile, approving and man-to-man, lifted Vin high. The fighting down here might not be as grand and glorious as that up north and east, but to follow a man like Ford—well, that was the kind of luck that usually fell to Darcy. As Vin left the drab building, it seemed to shine and his feet touched ground so lightly that he seemed to be in the clouds. He'd seen the cotton through, Pa would have the money to run the place another season; and now he could finally go to the war!

Two hours later Vin was heading southeast on the road to the King Ranch and Corpus Christi. The wind cut bitterly at Vin. He hunched his chin down beneath his turned-up collar and wondered why it seemed colder, traveling alone, than when he was with the train.

At least he wasn't staring down a line of flopping mule ears while the slow miles inched along. Vin patted the withers of his horse, a gaunt roan that looked as if someone had splashed alternate buckets of dirty red and white paint over its flea-bitten hide.

"Frijole's not beautiful," the army ostler had said. "But he's rugged."

"That makes two of us," Vin told the horse as they jogged on. "You've got a rugged pace, too. No wonder they wished you off on a greenhorn."

The day wore on, through a short stop by a waterhole where Frijole rested and Vin ate jerked beef and dry biscuit, through the afternoon, with no sight of a human. Vin talked more and more to his ungainly mount and by the time dusk fell and they stopped by a shallow creek, he was treating the horse like an old friend.

"Frijole," he said, unsaddling and bringing the hobbled horse some big bunches of prairie grass, "we aren't much for looks, but we'll make up for it with staying power, *verdad?*

How do you like my Spanish? I guess I really have to learn it now since I'm going to be here."

For the first time, Vin thought of Paco and the good chance they would soon meet again. Maybe he ought to take some knife lessons. Just in case Paco decided not to wait till the war was over. *Or I could learn to fiddle.* Munching at his cold food, Vin grinned at that idea.

It was his first night camp alone. Coon hunting back home, there'd always been Darcy, usually several other boys, and of course the hounds. Tonight Vin didn't dare even have a fire. He didn't want any more bandits!

Placing the saddle to block off as much wind as it could, he spread the saddle blanket and then wrapped up quickly in his single wool blanket and the tarp his supplies were rolled in.

How the wind moaned! Not a thing to stop its rush across the plains, not even a fence or lonesome tree. The cold had a piercing sting like that of an icy, wet cloth, but where the damp feel came from Vin had no idea for dust was in the air and burned his eyes and throat. Weary from the long ride, he slept fitfully, waking when he got rested enough to be aware of the cold, sleeping again when neither gritty wind, nor numb feet and face, nor jittery nerves could keep him awake. He was up early, glad to be through the miserable night.

By noon, Vin wished he could sleep. They'd struck no water so he singed some cactus for the horse whose name was now shortened to Holee. As it mouthed the green pads, Vin chewed more of the salty, tough, dried meat and blew on his hands for warmth.

"Holee," he said, mounting with a grimace, "it may not get cold enough here for a man to freeze, but it sure as the world makes him wish he could! Hump, *caballo!* Let's see how fast we can make it to the King."

RAIDED RANCHO

About mid-morning, Frijole pricked up his ears and snuffed. "Water, boy?" Vin asked. "I sure hope so!" In a few minutes they passed a stone outcropping with a muddy puddle beneath it that had once been a spring.

Dismounting, Vin forcibly shoved Frijole's muzzle aside while he half-filled his canteen, leaving all he could for the horse who snorted with eagerness as he literally sucked up the water. A dispirited dripping from the rock fed the pool but it would take hours to accumulate a gallon. As Vin rode on, he felt like a thief, for rail-thin cows stood with their bony flanks to the wind, and calves tugged hungrily at dry udders.

He passed near enough to one old brown cow to see her mouth was swollen so that the purplish tongue protruded from it like a gag, specked with cactus spines. Her eyes were glazed and she swayed as she walked. There was nothing Vin could do for her except pray it would rain, and he ached with pity, remembering what Brother Elkanah had said when they first reached the cactus flats.

" 'Cursed is the ground for thy sake . . . thorns and thistles shall it bring forth to thee.' " And later, after Eden, hadn't the earth cried out with the blood of the murdered Abel? Could it be the land, now, was sealing itself against men who still kept killing each other? Vin shrugged the notion aside. The wind and loneliness must be getting him! When there was war what could you do unless you were turned strange like Jare?

130

Let the Yankees have their own way, pass high tariff laws
so the South had to sell its cotton cheap to pay for high-priced
Northern manufactures? Let the Yankees pass laws that would
keep any slaveholding territory from becoming a state? Vin
snorted in indignation as he thought over how the North had
been goading the South for years now, blocking its growth by
laws favoring the industrialized North. Yankees carried on
about slavery, but everyone knew they had women and children working for starvation wages in their mills and factories.
Pa said if the North had stayed out of it, Southerners would
have freed their slaves eventually. Many already had, and
really, truly, Vin rather squirmed at the thought of what the
slaves sometimes had to endure—being sold, belonging to
another man, and—well, yes, there must be a little of that
cruelty from overseers and owners in a few places. But
granted it was wrong and should be ended, it should have
been left to the South to abolish it.

Slavery, Pa said, was a cause Northerners could wave flags
about and make fiery speeches against, but they were fighting
to keep the South tied to a government that no longer took the
South's needs into consideration. Hadn't the Southern states
helped form the Union, presumably for their good? Then,
when the Union became a tool of Yankees, serving them,
wasn't it fair that the Southern states withdraw? *We,* Vin
thought angrily, *would never have fought to keep the North
with us! Why didn't they let us go in peace?*

That day and the next three, Vin steadily traveled southeast. The slightly hilly country around San Antonio had long
ago yielded to brush and now to the flat coastal plains where
sand blew in constant torment. He and Frijole found enough
water to keep going, but Vin's mouth felt dry the second after
he finished drinking. Cattle here were even sadder than to the

west. They stood listlessly hunched against the wind as if it had blown them there. Polished by the wind-driven sand, skeletons whitened in the sun. Wolves and coyotes made easy prey of the weakened animals.

The morning of the fifth day, Vin sighted a pack of coyotes chasing a cow with a calf. Turning desperately, lunging at the attackers, she put up a game fight, but she couldn't face all directions at once. Two of her yellow-gray enemies dragged down the calf. Vin had loaded his carbine and rode forward, yelling, but he was too late. As the cow went for the pair on her calf, three caught her flanks while another took her throat. Bellowing, she tossed one yelping body on her horns, but she fell by her calf even as Vin fired.

Past noon that day he stiffened, rode in the saddle, eyes shielded to see better, then sighed with relief. Shimmering through the heat and dusty wind lay the ranch house of Santa Gertrudis, the lookout tower and cannon.

It looked plain beautiful to Vin. People, friends—real food and at least the sight of honest-to-goodness roofs, whether he was asked to sleep under them or not! He'd even be glad to see that uppity Estrella Riley. On all the way from San Antonio, Vin had seen exactly three people: a shepherd who'd hid behind some cactus at his approach, a farmer driving a wagon, and a horseman who'd ridden quickly past as if pleased to see Vin was a peaceful-looking boy who wasn't likely to rob him. Five days of that would make anyone feel sociable!

Yet as Vin neared the headquarters, a sense of disaster fastened on him. Surely people should be moving about, passing from commissary to smithy, from the corrals and sheds to the dwellings. And why weren't some cotton trains camped about? He caught a flash of motion from the corner of one eye—a small boy, naked except for a shirt, running into one of the thatched huts. Behind him, abandoned to the intruder, toddled a wailing little girl. Vin swung down from Frijole.

"Easy, honey," he called to the small lady; but she screamed the louder and her chubby brown legs drove like pistons.

"Oh, you're one of the teamsters!" Vin whirled towards the voice behind him, stared into the muzzle of a Colt that was slowly lowering, then at the lean face that had first welcomed him to the King Ranch almost three months ago.

"Silvano Vargas! I thought for a minute— Is something wrong?"

The *vaquero's* jaw set. "We had a bitter Christmas, *muchacho*. Yankees. They came at daybreak two days before Christmas and with sixty soldiers held the headquarters till Christmas Eve. They said Davis the *renegado* was camped on the Bóveda and would come down upon us, but I think they lied for he has not."

"Yanks *here?*" Vin had thought the distance to Fort Brown would make such a foray impracticable for the soldiers would have to cross a hundred and twenty miles of unfamiliar desert in order to get at the headquarters, and King had *vaqueros* who were no strangers to defending the lonely empire. "But where is Captain King?"

"Perhaps in Mexico, *quién sabe?* He heard the Yankees were coming but thought if he were gone, they wouldn't bother anyone else. Most of the fighting Kineños were off with Captain Richardson who has a company of Rangers, so we could not put up much of a defense. Captain King believed the soldiers, when they knew he wasn't here, would go away without harming anyone."

The blue eyes of Estrella Riley seemed to look at Vin. With a chill of dread, he asked slowly, "Was—somebody hurt?"

"They killed Francisco Alvarado as he stood on the porch of the great house, shouting that only a family was inside. They hunted through the rooms for the Captain, ripping the mattresses open with sabers, wrecking furniture, riding their horses across the floors. They took anything they wanted, clothes, blankets—like bandits, you understand, like animals from the *monte!* Silvano's voice shook and he spat into the dust. "All the men were put in a prison pen. The Yankees would even have put the Señor Hiram Chamberlain, old as he is, and a minister of the Presbyterians, in with us, but the lieutenant in charge became ashamed and left him free."

"The girl from Brownsville—Miss Riley?"

For the first time, as if her name was enough cause, Silvano smiled. "*Ay,* Estrella! She lives now in my house. *La Madama,* her father and her children, went by coach to San Patricio on Christmas day, for she is to have a baby soon, and it seemed likely that Davis would attack."

"Well, why in sam-hill didn't Estrella go, too?" Vin breathed in exasperation.

"*La Madama* urged her to, but Estrella wished to stay and see the great house set to rights and mend the torn coverlets and draperies. Also I believe it is in Estrella's mind to stay where she can know what is going on at Brownsville and with the cotton trade." Silvano frowned. "And why are you not with a wagon?"

Vin explained, ending, "How can I give my message to Captain King if you don't know where he is?"

"He will surely be back soon. In the meantime I will proceed with gathering the supplies and animals for I know my Captain would desire it. You must stay with us tonight. In the morning you may go to San Antonio and assure Colonel

Ford he will have his needs." Taking Frijole's bridle, Silvano nodded towards a *jacal* at the end of the row. "Go on to my house, you're weary. I'll see to your horse. *Caramba!* What beast is this? He looks like a Comanche bleached pale in spots!"

"But he travels well." Vin laughed to discover how swiftly he defended the horse he had thought ugly five days ago. "Is there grain?"

"I will find him some," Silvano promised. "The little Estrella will be glad to see you. She has often told us of Morrisey, The Snorer, and the fiddling lad."

If she said anything about me, it wasn't good, Vin thought. Not that he cared, of course. Yet he was baffled and a little angry at the way his feet hurried to the Vargas' home and then seemed to root a few paces from the door.

He shouldn't burst in without Silvano; he'd just go help get Frijole settled— He turned, heading for the corral.

"Vin!" Spinning about, he saw Estrella in the door. She— why, she looked all happy and sort of glowing. Then she frowned till he was sure he'd imagined her first expression. "I mean, Mister Clayburn. What are you doing here?"

"Military business," he said loftily. "You're the one who's out of place. Why didn't you go with Mrs. King?"

The girl's chin raised high above the prim collar. "Civilian business, Mister Clayburn."

"Yep," scoffed Vin. "Sewing up torn sofa pillows!" Spots of color burned in her cheeks, and small hands, held close to her sides, made fists.

"More than that, gringo! The cotton—" Biting her lip, she choked off the words.

Vin frowned. "Cotton? What could a girl have to do with that?"

"Oh!" she snapped, "come in the house and eat! I could have a better conversation with one of your mules!"

And two of a kind you'd be! Vin said under his breath, following her inside.

He met a full house. Seven children somehow played, slept, or ran about the single large room, which opened into two smaller ones. The oldest child was perhaps twelve, and the youngest was a tiny baby held in the warm curve of its mother's arm. Estrella spoke to this thin dark woman whose face, though tired, radiated kindness. Then, in English, Señora Vargas was introduced to Vin who bowed and murmured, *"Buenos días, señora."*

"Jare must have taught you," sniffed Estrella after an incredulous stare that gratified Vin immensely. But she brought him a bowl of warm beef stew, *tortillas,* and coffee, while the children, according to their ages, watched him with fascinated eyes or went on with their games.

Silvano came in. While Vin ate, he told briefly of the trip to Laredo, of Davis' expedition after Benavides and how the Gray Ghost had saved him and his friends, of Rip Ford and his own errand to the King Ranch.

"Ay, yes!" Indignant grief thrilled in Estrella's tone. "The war must go on, mustn't it? Does it matter that a peaceful man is shot before *La Madama's* door, that she must joggle across rough roads to a place where she can have her baby in safety? Does it matter that while men are off fighting their families must starve or be preyed on by thieves and Indians? Of course not! You men must have your cannons!"

She was being silly and unfair, but Vin felt like squirming. "I didn't start this war," he muttered, and winced at the limp excuse. Why didn't she behave as a girl should, doggone it?

"Of course you didn't! You just trotted off after the leaders like everyone else!" She snatched up his bowl. Vin thought she did it to vent her anger till she came back with more stew. Looking down at him, she made a face. "You smell worse than a goat! While you sleep I will wash those clothes. Those tears and holes, I'll mend them, too. Isn't your so glorious army going to give you a uniform?"

She didn't treat anything important with respect! Deep down, unadmitted even to himself, Vin had expected her to be impressed at his joining Rip Ford. Instead she acted as if he were in some child's make-believe.

"Pretty clothes don't win a war," he told her snubbingly.

"And neither does pneumonia or ripping one's skin on brambles!"

Grinning at Vin's discomfiture, Silvano said, "I have some clothes he can wear, Estrellita, while you are busy with those." She clapped her hands triumphantly while Vin glowered at his host.

"Bueno!" In swift Spanish, she issued orders to the children who scattered like quail. From one of the smaller rooms came thumping and bumping and a splashing sound while, with chatter, glances at Vin, and laughter, the children carried their assorted burdens into the room. When they had all emerged and stood at a polite distance surveying Vin, their eyes sparkled, and one little girl giggled before she dived blushing into her mother's skirts. "Now," said Estrella, "all is ready. Even in this drouth there is bath water for one so dirty, and soap."

"You will smell like a lily," Silvano encouraged, lips twitching.

With a reproachful look at him, Vin went into the small

room, pulled the curtain. Doggone, she was bossy! When she got married—if she ever did—it had better be to a Quaker like Jare who didn't believe in fighting.

Cleaner than he had been in—he shied away from an exact reckoning of the weeks, Vin lay down on the thong leather bed Señora Vargas indicated. Bones melting in the warmth of blankets, stomach comforted with good hot food, Vin sank luxuriously into sleep. As his eyes weighted shut, he saw Estrella, stitching at his clothes while she talked softly to the children. From oldest to youngest, they had gathered round her, eyes fixed on her curiously softened face.

It must be a fine story, Vin thought as his eyes closed all the way. *It's because of this the kids mind her; not just because she can use her tongue like a muleskinner.*

When he woke, he didn't know at first where he was. Warm little bodies lay around him so that he felt covered with arms and legs. The glowing fire showed Silvano already dressed, fitting on his spurs, while Señora Vargas and Estrella placed food on the table. Vin, fully clothed in Silvano's things, gently worked his way out from beneath three nestling children, and stood up, stretching.

"What a sleep! But you should have rolled me off on a blanket instead of letting me keep the bed all night."

"You'll have plenty of ground-sleeping," Silvano laughed. "I'll grain and saddle your horse while you eat." He went out. Estrella nodded towards one of the small rooms.

"Your own clothes are in there."

She had, Vin found, reinforced the elbows, seat, and knees, with soft leather, which was lucky since the cloth had about worn through in those places. "Thanks," he told her as he laid Silvano's garb on a chest.

"It is nothing," she said, translating the Spanish formula, but her mouth curved with pleasure. "Now eat with interest, for it is far to San Antonio."

Beef, fried beans with onions and cheese, crisp *tortillas*— Vin needed no urging. He figured this might well be his last woman's cooking till after the war. Estrella sat down across from him.

"So you serve with the Colonel Ford." She sighed a little, seeming to look back. "I remember when he was married, in Brownsville, almost three years ago. Reverend Chamberlain, *La Madama's* father, performed the ceremony, and guests came from both sides of the Rio Grande. The Cortina trouble had been settled and the border was, for it, peaceful. Happy days—"

Vin, stealing a glance at her, felt a pang of sympathy for this girl who seemed so grown-up and domineering. Since Ford's wedding, her mother had died and another war had come to the Rio land, leaving her homeless. No wonder she had grown a prickly coating.

When he could eat no more, Vin rose. He thanked Señora Vargas in what he thought rather passable Spanish, then turned to Estrella. "You want to stay on here?"

"Of course."

"Do you need any money?"

She shook her head. "I," she announced proudly, "have a partnership with Captain King." Vin stared.

"You? With *him?*" Thinking of the burly, black-bearded captain, Vin laughed outright. "You mean he sells the things you make? Or buys them for his trade?"

"Neither!" She snatched up a parcel from the table. "Here's some lunch. Now go. I don't need your money or amusement!" Silvano, who had poked his head in the door, whistled as Vin escaped.

"*Ay*, a *chili* temper! But a good cook and most clever with the sewing. You could marry worse."

Vin, mounting, almost lost his stirrup-hold from shock. Safely up, he grinned at Silvano, spoke just loud enough for Estrella to hear. "*Gracias*, Silvano. You've reminded me something could be worse than losing a war. I'll give Colonel Ford your promise about the supplies." Noticing that Silvano was staring north, Vin turned to look.

"A wagon," he said. "All by its lonesome, too."

"Bad weather and bad times for that," frowned Silvano. His voice sharpened. "Do my eyes trick me, or is one of the teamsters wearing a shawl around his head?"

"That," said Estrella, "is not a shawl. It is a bonnet such as gringo women wear—and look, can't you see it is a woman? She has skirts!"

"The driver is a Negro," Vin made out. "And that's a Negro woman in the middle. She's wearing the kind of scarf Aunt Rachel used to—" The words broke off in his throat. It couldn't be! Yet—

Spinning Frijole, Vin rode fast towards the wagon. His heart pounded so high in his chest he could hardly breathe, wind stung his eyes till they watered and his vision blurred. But he knew the small woman in the black bonnet and dress, he knew the ebony faces of Aunt Rachel and Uncle Jess, though his mind screamed they couldn't truly be here, over a thousand miles from home. As he drew alongside in a halfcircle, saw his mother's arms reach out to him, heard her cry with tears and laughter, the color of her garb struck him.

Mother didn't like black; "that horrid crow color" she called it. For church and solemn affairs she wore dark gray and blue. Only for a funeral would she put on the black, high-necked dress she wore now. And a black bonnet? For Mother, whose love of bright colors fought a constant battle with what she believed a lady should be seen in?

Hurdling from the saddle, Vin helped his mother from the wagon seat, felt her tears and kisses and had a hard time of it not to blubber. It had been so long. And she was smaller; or maybe he had grown. But when they finally stepped back to look at each other, Vin, with a distinct painful shock saw her as a person, a woman—not simply as his mother, though she would always be that, too. Their embrace had knocked her bonnet off, showing a streak of white at either temple, in the hair that had been black as Darcy's when Vin last saw her. The fine lines around her eyes and mouth had deepened. Her eyes were spirited and darkly beautiful as ever, but the lids seemed bruised and heavy.

"Vin!" she gasped, catching his hands again. "What luck to find you here! And you look so well, so healthy. I—I was afraid—" She caught him to her and began to cry.

"What—why—?" he began and could get no further. Dread choked him. He looked up in appeal at Aunt Rachel who had so often, when he was little and hurt himself, picked him up and crooned to him till the pain left.

But she, like his mother, was a separate, new person now, an older, wearier woman whose face was deeply wrinkled, and who had begun silently to rock herself, arms clasped in front of her. Vin glanced at Uncle Jess, who gazed back in compassion and mute sympathy, wet his lips several times, and spoke reluctantly.

"Poor Mistuh Vin, your daddy is dead, and your mama

here, she fotched her nice things and the famous ole fiddle for to be sold and get medicines. And Mistuh Da'cy, he's lost an arm in the war and gone off somewhere all bitter into the heart 'cause he cain't be a surgeon now." The fuzzy white head shook sadly. "Troubles, Mistuh Vin, just everywhere troubles."

Pa—dead?

Vin's breath doubled painfully as if it would burst his skin, and he gulped for air; then he felt numb, and light and cold. It was too much to realize. Even as he held his mother and was glad he could try to comfort her, he felt the grief sinking deep, deep into him, knew it would flood over him later. And there would be no one, not Mother or Aunt Rachel, to hold him and talk softly. However beloved, they were *persons* now, and he was alone, inside himself. But Darcy? An arm lost?

When his mother's weeping began to subside, Vin said gently, "Tell me about it."

The sound of his voice seemed to brace her. Drawing back though still holding his hand, she told him what had happened.

They had scarcely gotten Darcy's letter saying that he had joined the cavalry and was fighting in Virginia when a letter from his commanding officer told them Darcy had been seriously wounded during a gallant charge. An arm had been amputated, but Darcy was recovering and should be on his way home soon since he could no longer fight. The commander had hinted that Darcy was hurt more seriously in spirit and mind than in his body.

"Your father had to stay at the farm," Mother went on, "but I was worried for Darcy. There's never been any telling what he'd do in a disappointment, so I traveled to the hospital in Virginia to bring him home. He wasn't there, Vin! The attendants said as soon as he could manage alone, he left and all he would say was that he wasn't going home, a cripple, till he had plenty of money to support himself and his family— and if he got killed trying to get it, he didn't care because if he couldn't be a one-armed doctor, he wasn't going to be a one-armed beggar."

Wincing, physically sick for his brother, Vin waited for the gentle, worn voice to finish. Each word hit him like the blow of an invisible hammer till his knees were so weak he was surprised he was still standing.

Returning home without her son, his mother found the farm and outbuildings charred to the ground. Behind the partially burned house in the family graveyard was a new mound. Union guerillas, thieves, really, had come down on the farm late one Sunday, six of them. Trying to lure Pa, Aunt Rachel and Uncle Jess outside, the raiders fired barn, sheds, stables, fodder stacks, woodpiles, but when they swooped towards the house, the three defenders stood them off, killing two.

Enraged at this, the others rushed the house with fire brands and rifles. One pitched from his saddle, thrusting his torch under the stoop as he died, but the others had enough. They circled back, driving off the cattle, and disappeared. But Pa had taken two wounds from the last charge and died that night, in spite of all Aunt Rachel and Uncle Jess could do. They had buried him, done what they could to restore the farm, and waited for their mistress. Darcy, even with one arm, would have been heaven's own gift to the desolated farm. But—

Mother bit her lip, got her voice firmly under control. "I had already decided something at that hospital, Vin. Dozens of boys no older than Darcy, some young as you, lay untended and dirty, without even enough food and—and I heard them take off the leg of one man who'd developed gangrene. They had to do it *without drugs,* son, without even that pitiful small mercy! It was the same with Darcy. That's what I've dreamed about, that's what devils me even more than what happened to your father; we were home in comfort while Darcy went through torture a little morphine could have saved him. I vowed in that hospital to sell every luxury I had for medicines to send to the hospitals." She nodded at the wagon, a ramshackle affair patched together with rope, nails, and bits of newer boards. "The Louis Quatorze sofa's in there, the bedposts, those two Italian tables, my silverplate, the old clock." Her tone wavered but she went on. "Most important, there's the Stradivarius. I really feel it belongs to Darcy, and I'd like his consent, but there's no telling where he is."

Though Darcy was the oldest son and the one who played the violin, Vin felt a pang. It hadn't even occurred to his mother that *he* might want it. Then he felt guilty for being jealous. He said slowly, "I don't understand, Mother. Why did you bring the things way off down here?"

"To sell them, as I said."

"Here?" Vin swept his arm around the brushland. Uncle Jess chuckled and even Mother smiled.

"I planned on taking the wagon to San Antonio. If I couldn't sell them there, I hoped one of the merchants who trade into Mexico with England and France might buy them. With Yankees holding New Orleans, I didn't know of any other place to sell them. No one back home is buying antiques these days!"

That was true. But for Mother who believed in "leaving men's business to men" to come all this wild, dangerous way with only two old servants— Supposing they had met Jims or Union irregulars?

"You were lucky this far," Vin said grimly. "But the Union

commander at Fort Brown is encouraging all kinds of bandits and guerillas to waylay travelers. He wants to stop wagons between San Antonio and the border completely, choke off our supply line. You can't go any further."

Mother's head snapped back. She started to speak, thought a moment, and said slowly, "You don't think we could get the wagon to the border in case I couldn't sell the things in San Antonio?"

"I don't think you could and I can't let you try it! No, Mother, we'll just unload the wagon here at the ranch and perhaps Captain King can sell it for you." Silvano, who had ridden up and waited a polite distance away, nodded at this, but Mother shook her head.

"No. Till there's the hard cash for medicines in my hand, I'm not leaving these things. They're too precious. I'd rather sell my blood if anybody'd pay for it."

Vin guessed a woman might very well feel that way about belongings that had been handed down in her family since before the French Revolution, brought over the seas at great cost to remain a heritage. Still, with neither Darcy nor Pa here to stop such goings-on, he, Vin, would have to. He cleared his throat. Mother was no more used to being told what to do than he was used to telling her.

"You can't go on, Mother. I won't let you."

Her eyes flashed. For a minute she seemed unable to speak from pure shock. But gradually, a smile softened her mouth.

"Then, Vin, you must take the wagon."

A STRANGE WAGON

Frozen in his tracks, Vin stared at his mother. He take charge of the wagon? Now, when he was finally free to join Rip Ford?

"Oh, no," he said, talking against luck and time and conscience as much as against his mother. "You can't ask me to do that! It—it's not fair!"

Her shoulders moved tiredly. "Then don't ask me not to. It will be done, Vin, and by one of us."

"But, Mother, I'm all set to join the army in San Antonio just as quick as I can get back there. Colonel Ford needs volunteers. And—"

He couldn't talk on against her eyes. Breathing heavily, he looked at the fine white dust, hated it passionately along with fate and the rest of this desolate hard-scrabble country where nothing worked right.

"You—" Evidently his mother had received a blow, too. "You want to get in the army? After Darcy? Vin, please— why, you're not even seventeen!"

"Plenty of boys younger than I are fighting. I wanted to go as bad as Darcy but I stayed with that old cotton instead and now—" He bit off what he had started to say: that he was old enough for hustling mules through a desert and bandits and that it seemed to be only when he *wanted* to do something that he was suddenly a kid.

His mother was silent for what seemed a long time, as if

146

she were arguing inside herself. At length she said, "If you have to fight, if you feel it in you that you must or be less a man the rest of your life, then I can't ask you to stay with the wagons. It's hard for me to realize you're not a little boy. Obey your conscience, Vin."

That was just the trouble. Conscience, duty, pulled him two directions. He knew that getting a large supply of drugs for wounded men was more important, honestly, than the fighting he could do. But, oh, he was tired of feeling like a conscript-dodger! He looked worriedly at his mother.

"Will you let me try to sell the things through Captain King?"

"No. We came safe this far. We can go the rest of the way."

What made it different was that before Vin hadn't known the risk she was running; now he would, so it was put squarely on him to decide. For a split second he wished he *hadn't* met her, that he could have joined Ford securely believing she was safe at home, and was immediately shamed even before she spoke in that gentle, loving way which was his earliest memory.

"Don't worry, Vin. We will both do what we think we should and not reproach each other."

Boys of sixteen who are planning to join an army don't cry but Vin felt dangerously close to it. Either that or saying something hateful and mean. With a physical effort, he waited till he could trust his voice, till he could say what he should, and no more.

"It's bad enough that I can't ride guard for you going back home, Mother. I can't let you go further south. First I'll have to take a message to Colonel Ford, and the wagon can stay at this ranch with friends I trust till I come back for it."

So it was decided. All the while as he escorted his mother

to Silvano's and watched Señora Vargas and Estrella make the travelers heartily welcome, Vin's heart grew heavier and heavier till it seemed to weigh as much as that wretched wagon he now had to dispose of. It was a blessing that he had to make some arrangements for his mother, Aunt Rachel, and Uncle Jess. Silvano took the responsibility of fitting out a light buggy for their return trip, payment for which would come out of the cotton money Mark was keeping for the Clayburns.

"I'll send the rest of the money to you by Brother Elkanah," Vin told his mother. She shook her head.

"Have Brother Elkanah take only enough to pay our mortgage. You spend the rest on medicines."

"Where shall I send them?"

"To the infirmary run by Miss Sally Tompkins in Richmond. I met her when I went to hunt for Darcy and told her I'd come back to work in the hospital after I sold these things."

"Work in a hospital?" Vin thought with revulsion of the cough-filled, gloomy infirmary in San Antonio. A hospital full of wounded men would be a hundred times worse. "Mother, you're doing enough, giving up all your heirlooms, coming off down here with them! Please go home!" He thought of the most powerful inducement he could. "Darcy may turn up any time but if no one's there, you know he'll drift."

Estrella said softly, "It would be so hard for you, *madama*." They had liked each other right off. Now Mother smiled at the girl.

"Not as hard as staying home while my two sons are gone. After the war we can all go home, build back our burnt places and harvest and plant. Life can be happy again. But now to serve is more important."

The small dark girl who hated war looked thoughtful. Vin wondered where she would go after the war. She had no home now, no family. With a sudden lift of her head, she turned to Vin's mother.

"May I go with you, *madama?*"

It was Mother's turn to protest. "Child, it's no place for a young girl. Your parents—"

"Are dead. So I am really a good one to go, you see, I wouldn't be missed." Her cheeks flushed with excitement and blue eyes earnestly implored the older woman.

"Are you crazy?" Vin blurted before he even knew what he was saying. "I'd miss—I mean, Silvano and the children and the *señora* here would miss you."

Estrella looked pleased but she said coldly, "It is not your affair. *Madama,* please! I am strong and I could take my sewing machine to make clothes for the sick."

"I don't understand, my dear," said Mother. "Why should you want to go so far and do such hard work?"

In her lap, Estrella's hands were clasped tight. Her eyes glistened as she said in a low voice, "I want to be to some person important. I want to belong somewhere, and I like you very much, *madama.* If I go with you now, perhaps after the war I can go with you to your home. I would be useful, I promise!"

For proud fiery Estrella to say this quite took Vin off balance. He thought, *If she wants to stay with my mother, she must like me a little bit.* Somehow this made him ridiculously pleased. Mother glanced at him, gave a humorous lift of her shoulders.

"This seems to be the day of decisions," she said. "Yes, Estrella, you may come with me, and be very welcome."

Shortly afterwards as Vin started for San Antonio, Estrella called to him, smiling, "You needn't worry about your mother, Vin. You know I'm resourceful!" He knew, too, that she was pretty, and he was glad she would be with his mother the next hard months. But what a muddle it was!

Mother, two old colored people, and Estrella, heading for Richmond, toward the war, while he had to go away from it! And how would he explain to Rip Ford? Well, maybe he could sell the Stradivarius and furniture in San Antonio and still join up. He hoped!

Pushing Frijole against the bitter wind, he reached San Antonio five days later, having met Mark and the other teamsters on the way. Explaining about his mother and changed plans, Vin asked Brother Elkanah to pay the mortgage, kept out enough cash to pay for Frijole and necessities, and left the rest of the cotton money with Mark. Mark had gloomy news of Bragg's defeat at Missionary Ridge and Vin glumly thought as he reported to Rip Ford that the year of 1864 was off to a bad start. How long could this war go on?

Ford, though, acted as if it were just beginning. "Ah!" he greeted, shaking hands, "Here's our volunteer. What word have you from Captain King?"

Vin told of the Christmas raid on the ranch, Silvano's assurance of supplies. Then he came to the words that stuck in his throat.

"I—I'm afraid I'm not a volunteer after all, sir." Tell the whole long story? Seem to beg for sympathy and understanding? As a chill, alert look sharpened Ford's expression, Vin cut off abruptly. "Something's come up that I have to attend to personally, Colonel. I hope to get it out of the way in time to join your force, but it may take longer."

Ford seemed to be carefully keeping emotion from his voice. "Of course you aren't of an age for conscription yet," he said drily, switching his attention to his papers. "Thanks for being my messenger at any rate, and good day."

Strange that such a polite dismissal could smart more than a slap in the face. Flushing, Vin wheeled and left.

Colonel Ford hadn't even said he hoped Vin would be able to volunteer later. Probably the tough old border soldier thought Vin had gotten cold feet. *I'll get right back to the King Ranch,* Vin promised himself grimly. *Mark and Jare should be ready to leave by then and we'll bring our wagons into San Antonio fast as possible. If I can just sell the things without going to the border!* Though it was mid-afternoon, he paid at the quartermaster's for Frijole, bought some food from a street vendor as he passed through town, and started the trip that night. He was getting mighty sick of this particular stretch of desert!

Sure enough, when he rode into the main works of the ranch, Jare, Roncador, and Mark were stowing bales into the wagons, aided by Silvano and several *vaqueros.* After the first greetings, Mark gave Vin a crooked grin, raised an eyebrow.

"Reckon you can guide us into San Antonio?"

Vin shuddered. Roncador slapped him on the shoulder. "Cheer up, lad! You can conduct tours through this tropic paradise after the war—make your fortune!" Vin managed a faint laugh. He knew their joshing was meant to help him but he wasn't in the temper for it. Now what was Jare, with a shine in his eyes, so churned up about? He came to Vin, almost stammering with delight.

"Vin, I got to play the fiddle—the Stradivarius! It's wonderful, thee can't imagine. We got here the day thy mother left and she gave me leave to handle it!"

Vin humphed, and jealousy stirred in him again. Jare got to play all the Clayburn fiddles. He, Vin, had never even fingered the Stradivarius because it was taken for granted in the family that it would one day be Darcy's. *Darcy with his arm gone—how would he play now?* That didn't bear thinking about. Vin seemed to see his brother's face in a flash of longing and grief. Where was he? Would he never come home again? And at the same time, Vin resentfully felt that if Darcy hadn't been hurt, mother would never have seen the hospital and brought all this stuff down here for him to have to drag to market. Yet—men, like Darcy, enduring surgery with no ease for pain? Oh, no, this should be done, it was as high a service as anything could be.

Only why do I have to do it?

"Well, you'd better enjoy the fiddle while it's here," Vin said abruptly. "I'm going to sell it fast as I can."

Jare said, "It is brave of thy mother." He added softly, "And very brave of thee, Vin."

"Shucks," Vin scoffed, "I can't play it."

"No. But thee wished to join Colonel Ford."

"Maybe I still can," said Vin almost savagely. He turned his horse over to one of Silvano's young ones and started at once to help load the wagons, working feverishly. He grudged each hour till they could leave. The sooner they reached San Antonio the better chance he would have of disposing of his peculiar load in time to soldier.

The bitter north wind screamed at them all the way to San Antonio. Vin was so wild with impatience that it seemed to him they were frozen puppets moving with stiff, brittle halts and jerks across a boundless stage of sand and twisted brush. Frequently their meals came from cows who were staggering to their knees with starvation and which would surely have died anyway. At San Antonio the three cotton wagons were to pick up extra teamsters hired by Captain King, but for now Jare,

Roncador, and Mark each had to manage a team alone while Vin wrestled with his own odd freight.

Driving through the day with hands so chapped and sore they sometimes bled and stuck to the reins, Vin would think the night halt would never come. Then when they stopped he would think despairingly of the scant twelve or so miles they had done that day and would be in a fever to start again.

Besides, the nights were far from restful. Though they put the wagons around their camp for protection from bandits and wind, these did little to break the piercing gales, and the mules were miserable from lack of water. Vin had left Frijole at the King and was glad the weirdly colored horse was being spared this trip back.

The noon stops had to be extra long so that enough cactus could be singed to feed the beasts. At night this pulpy fare was supplemented with precious grain from the ranch. After the teams were fed, their drivers huddled around a carefully coaxed and tended fire, which spluttered protests at the wet sticks and brush it had to live on. As quickly as they could, the shivering Missourians fixed supper—jerked beef stew or fresh beef from some unfortunate cow, a grind of herbs and roots that served for coffee, and Roncador's sour dough bread.

By then they were thawed out enough to spread their blankets close to one another, hunch their backs to the cold, and try to sleep. All but Jare.

He played the fiddle. Yes, he did. Night after night, though his fingers were scabbed and his touch made clumsy. He would sit by the sullen fire and bend his head to the violin, humming softly. He played many tunes but mostly, because Mark and Roncador asked for them, songs like *Dixie, Goober Peas,* and *Bonnie Blue Flag.*

"It's a Confederate fiddle," Mark said one night, laughing,

"For all its foreign name." He was speaking of the Stradi-varius, though Jare didn't always play it.

He alternated. One night, Darcy's fiddle, the next, the Strad. *As if,* thought Vin scornfully, *he doesn't want to hurt either's feelings!* Jare was just funny enough to think that way, too.

Vin would lie on the pesky ground and try to stop his ears, annoyed with both Jare and himself. Anxious as he was to be rid of the violin and antiques so he could join Ford, he still hated to give up things that had been in their family long enough to seem part of it. He should be the one giving the Strad this loving farewell, this last time of music. But he couldn't play. He could only hear Jare, worry about his mother, Estrella, and Darcy, and wish it would hurry up and be day so the wagons could lumber their piddling little dis-tance before the next night. The others seemed to guess how he felt for they let him pretty much alone.

It took two grinding weeks to reach San Antonio. Their only excitement had been a brush with two bandits who had thrown a few shots at them from antiquated muskets and van-ished fast when they discovered the teamsters had rifles and could shoot. They got to the city about noon, made camp at King's depot, and ate. Vin bolted his food. Maybe, this very day, he could sell his load. Before he brought the things in, though, he had better find a potential buyer. As he started towards the business district he called to Jare, who was pol-ishing the Stradivarius.

"Want to come along?"

Jare hesitated, said with real regret, "Thank thee, no, Vin. If thee don't mind I'd like to stay with the fiddle."

"Suit yourself," said Vin, and stalked off. Jare took on as if that fiddle were human! And it wasn't even his.

Vin wandered through the streets, bought a mouth-watering handful of quince candy from a street vendor, and finally came to a shop that had a great many curious things in its window, including some musical instruments, many knives, fans, fancy vests and shawls, jewelry, and firearms. As Vin went in he cast a hungry look at the beautiful knives and decided he'd try to buy one. He had a little money out of the cotton proceeds.

With Vin's Spanish and the shopkeeper's English, they managed to understand each other.

"I have sorrow," the owner said, "but the furniture I cannot handle. For the fiddle I could give you a little but not what it is worth. You had better go to Mr. Carpenter. Yes, that is good! He deals in valuable things and has connections in Mexico and even Europe." And he told Vin how to find the office.

"Thousand thanks," said Vin. He was turning to leave when his gaze struck on a knife that made wanting any other knife impossible.

Fourteen inches long, almost two inches wide at the guard, the blade was razor sharp in front while the back of the pointed section had two inches honed fine enough to rip. On the black walnut handle was a silver plate engraved in a small, elegant script. Vin whistled.

"This knife, *señor*—what does the writing say?"

The proprietor smiled. "You like it, *pero no?* It says, and truly, *'I am as good as the man who wields me.'* " He twanged the tip of the blade with his thumb. "Hear, it rings like a bell! It is made of the same steel as the brave Colonel Bowie's famous knife."

Vin doubted that. Imitations of the Bowie were everywhere and lots of Missourians used them. After all, the maker of the great original had been next door, in Arkansas. But this knife appealed to him on its own merits. He bargained a while and left for Carpenter's with it sheathed proudly at his belt.

Mr. Carpenter, a thin, tall man with sandy hair and mustache, stopped drumming his fingers on his desk and considered aloud. "I can dispose of the furniture to customers who have asked me to watch for certain antiques, and my price will be good, I assure you. The Stradivarius—" He spread his hands. "That would be a speculation. It might take me years to sell it so I can't pay much, not a fraction of what it would bring from a person who really wanted it. My advice is to take it to Laredo, and then down the Mexican bank to Matamoros. Seek out foreign merchants and businessmen. You will almost certainly get twenty times what it'll fetch in San Antonio."

Go all that way? Vin's heart jackknifed like a hooked fish. "Sir, please—" he stopped, biting his lip. No, he couldn't take a trifling sum for it, not after what it meant to Mother and the agonized men the extra money would provide drugs for. He made a last desperate try to evade the journey. "Sir, perhaps you could sell it to those foreigners?"

Carpenter shrugged. "My boy, with the border in its present state I prefer not to send unsold articles of value down there. For me it would not be worth the risk and trouble. I will not cheat you, but neither shall I practice poor business procedures." He began drumming at the desk again, glanced impatiently at a sheaf of bills and papers. Vin swallowed, blinked at the sting in his eyes, as he moved towards the door.

"You will take the furniture, silver, and jewels?"

"Of course, of course! Didn't I say so? That is, if their condition is what you claim. I shall come in the morning to see, and if all is satisfactory, we'll conclude our bargain." Carpenter cast Vin a more friendly look. "I am honestly giving you good counsel on the violin," he said. "But if you want to look around San Antonio in the chance of a better offer, I'll give you some addresses."

"Yes, please!" breathed Vin. A few minutes later, he left the office tightly clutching a list of merchants.

If only one would take the Strad! Surely they would! To a big business like Mr. Carpenter's the transaction might not be worth the trouble and risk, but for a more gambling-natured man it might be a challenge. Or so Vin hoped.

At sundown, footsore, hungry, and disgusted, Vin found his way back to camp. Jare looked up from helping Roncador with the cooking.

"Any luck?" he asked, and sounded, at least to Vin's prejudiced ears, as if he wanted Vin to still have the fiddle on his hands.

"It appears you'll get to play that old Strad all the way to the border." Vin sounded nastier than he intended, tried to turn it into a joke by forcing a laugh. "I think I can sell the other stuff but to get anything much from the fiddle, I'll have to try in Matamoros."

"Well, lad," consoled Roncador, "we'll wrap it up good and stick it in one of the cotton wagons. Then in Laredo we'll figure out a way for you to travel with a group big enough for protection."

Handing Vin a plate, Mark said briskly, "I'm sure enough glad to have another good mule-whacker. Captain King has eight wagons ready to go but can't find enough reliable teamsters. Even if we have to start short-handed, we need to leave day after tomorrow."

"The sooner the better," Vin muttered. His plate clanged

against his knife as he bent for some stew. Roncador jumped back in pretended fright.

"Where'd you get that weapon? You aim to butcher cows with it?"

Stung, Vin retorted, "It's for fighting," and thought immediately of Paco. Use the knife on someone? No, he'd hate that. He guessed it was mostly for looks. It didn't take Mark's amused glance to tell him that was kid stuff, but Vin was drubbed if he'd take it off now. Filling his plate, he retired to a wagon wheel and chewed morosely. Another whole day before they'd even get started! And then days and days of urging flop-eared, balky mules along through the biting sand, and nights and nights of listening to Jare play the fiddle that was the cause of it all!

Choking on a piece of stringy beef, Vin coughed violently and gave up eating. How he hated mule-whacking, how he hated cotton—and how tired he was of doing what he ought instead of what he wanted!

Mr. Carpenter came next morning early, approved his purchases, had them carefully rewrapped and transferred to his wagon. Vin, young and male though he was, felt a pang as he watched the sofa, the old carved clock, the great bed posts, and the Italian tables being closed from view for the last time. He had lived with them all his life before leaving Missouri, and their sale brought the realization sharply to him that his home would never be the same again, even if he and Darcy and Mother and Estrella did all go back, even if the South won. Pa was—*yes, say it, dead. But then think on past before you cry*. And the Clayburns who went home could not be the same people, especially not Darcy who couldn't be a surgeon now.

And where was Darcy? Where had he gone to try to find the wealth he seemed to need now before he could go home? Vin shook his head, unable to imagine Darcy as he must be now. For Darcy had always done what he wanted, and there were so many things the loss of his arm would bar him from. Vin didn't think any amount of money could make it up and it made him sick in his heart to think of his brother.

"Now," said Mr. Carpenter, drumming on the wagon seat since his desk wasn't handy. "I suppose you want your money in gold rather than paper and I'm impressed enough by the sacrifice of your family to oblige. You'll need gold to buy those drugs anyway." He counted out a stack of coins, the hard metal scarce in the South, and dumped them into a leather bag. "Here you are," he said, holding out his hand. "Good luck to you." He looked at the Strad Jare was holding. "It's a real shame to have to sell that. Sorry I couldn't help you but you'll do much better in Mexico."

Returning the handclasp, Vin thanked him, and turned quickly so he wouldn't see Mother's things going away. Jare wrapped up the fiddle and said casually, "Let's go see Tía Luisa, Vin. I think she is the kind of lady who will always have cookies for hungry travelers." Though Vin suspected this excursion was thought up to lift his spirits, he was too depressed to stand on pride.

"Let's go," he said.

OVER WILD HORSE DESERT

When they came back from visiting Tía Luisa, who had both cakes and cookies and a warm welcome, several strange men lounged around the camp. They were the new teamsters, all King's representative had been able to find. Mark introduced the boys to them. Diego Cruz and Raul de León were weathered men in their sixties who spoke courteously and went back to their shuck cigarettes. Warren Manners had a long, sad, likeable hound-face with ears practically as large. His cinnamon whiskers were spotted with white as well as the dark stains of tobacco. The gaze of the last man, Clance Cowan, grew bright as he saw Vin's knife. He was long and raw-boned with yellowish hair and handlebar mustaches, and his eyes took on a golden sheen as he flipped his finger towards the Bowie.

"What's that weighin' you down, laddie?"

"Nothing is," said Vin.

But Cowan was not to be squelched. He lightly appropriated the knife, balanced it like a scholar examining a rare and long-hunted book. "Some toad-stabber. Know how to use it?"

Ears burning, Vin said "I can't throw it, but—"

"You can't throw a Bowie," snorted Cowan. From a scabbard slung at the back of his neck beneath his fringed leather shirt, he produced an Arkansas toothpick. Vin had seen them before.

160

Straight-bladed with a vicious double edge, they were more
dagger than knife. "Look." Clance Cowan threw it by the butt
so that it spun, rotated in the air, and buried an inch deep in a
wagon where it vibrated crazily, light glancing off it in
streams. Pulling it free, Clance thrust it back into its sheath.
"This'n will serve for handwork, too. But Bowies are purely
for fighting." He squinted in a friendly way down his long narrow nose. "If you're going to carry one, youngster, learn its
use. Or it'll dig your grave."

"Some troops use those Bowies for bayonets," drawled
Warren.

Clance grunted. "Place for a Bowie is in your hand. Tell
you what, while we've some spare time, I'll give you a lesson."

Vin was not so sure he wanted one. He didn't know to avoid
it, though, without seeming afraid, so he nodded and said,
"Fine." Before drawing his own weapon, Clance showed Vin
how to hold the Bowie, thumb against the guard, pointed out
and upward.

"The idea," Clance explained, getting out his own knife and
assuming a careless but wary stance, "is to take my thrusts on
the back of your blade and turn them out and away. At the
same time, keep your point aimed at my body and be ready for
an opening. All right now! Get your feet wider apart for balance. Right foot in front a bit more—head and body back.
Good!"

Vin hesitated. Those knives were mighty sharp.

"Don't be ginger," Clance exhorted, swaying lightly.
"You're not going to hurt me and I won't nick you."

Trying to hold his stance, Vin thrust forward. Clance easily
turned the blow, parried Vin's next.

"Forget these stories about overhand strokes," Clance
warned. "Get your knife up that high and you're dead before

you know it. Go for the soft parts, don't aim at the head or get your knife tangled up in a collarbone or rib. You could be killed while trying to work it loose. And remember that with a Bowie you have a cutting blade on both edges. You parry me now."

The words were barely past Clance's teeth when Vin was dazzled by the blade feinting in and down. It stopped an inch short of his belt. Frozen, muscles of his stomach tight as wires, Vin watched the blade drop, flash again. Sucking in air, Vin turned the stroke on his knife so that it slid harmlessly into the thumb guard. Even trusting Clance, it was chilly business to stare down that foot of cold steel. Vin did his best to thwart that blue-silver flashing, but his breath came in painful stabbing gasps after a few minutes. More and more often Clance checked the point tinglingly short of a vulnerable spot.

Roncador, who with the others, was looking on, lumbered forward. "Go a round with me, Clance, and let the boy see how it is," Vin was glad to turn the Bowie over to the cook.

What followed was an education. Roncador was out of practice, but the feel came back to him fast. He must once have been a brilliant knife-man. Thrust and recover, feint and parry, like dancing, like fencing, a rhythm of sinews and danger. Soon their breathing came labored and hard; Roncador sounded like his nighttime snoring. At last, the tempo slowed, stopped completely by mutual consent. Though it was January, both dripped sweat.

"Say," panted Clance, laughing, "for a Missourian you're pretty good."

"Not bad yourself for a young kid," Roncador shot back. "Now you've had fair warning it's not safe to grouch about my cookin' let's go eat it!"

They rolled next morning, eight wagons with only a driver apiece. Vin's crazy-quilt vehicle had been replaced by a stout King wagon. Packed carefully, by Jare, between the bales and the cover tarp was the Stradivarius. Vin did believe if there'd been no other swaddling available, Jare would have used his blankets and slept bare!

Except for the dwindled number of teamsters, it was almost like starting again from Missouri, and that was how Vin felt, too. He had found out that Ford was still collecting men and supplies. Could he, Vin, in any wild fortune, get the fiddle sold and have time to get in on Ford's mysterious expedition?

He had to hope so, but the hope and its urgency nagging against the slow pace made him edgy, even if he hadn't sickened at the dozens of gaunt cattle they saw.

Dying on their feet, ripped at by the furious north wind, the pitiful creatures did not always fight off the coyotes who ran up in threes and fours to drag at them. It was a terrible winter and even Galveston Bay was said to be frozen over. Vin wondered about mother, Estrella, Aunt Rachel and Uncle Jess. They would be facing the bitter north but perhaps—he hoped!—the trees and hilly lands would cut the blast from them. It was bad when women and old folks had to endure such a journey. Still, though he wished they were all safe in a warm house, Vin felt stern pride in them. They certainly seemed more heroic than he did, that was sure!

After they corraled that night and tended their mules, Vin ate and rolled at once into his blankets. When Jare began softly teasing the fiddle, Vin gave a loud, obvious, rude sigh.

The fiddle stopped. Vin lay still, shamed yet angry. Clance said in a stage whisper, "Now what got his nose all out of joint? Me, I'd admire to hear some fiddlin'."

"Go ahead and hear it then," Vin retorted. "Can't a body

draw a breath if he's a mind to?" He rolled into a tighter bunch, cut off from the others by his own ill temper, knowing he had behaved like a spoiled baby.

Clance wouldn't let it rest, though. He said thoughtfully, "Anyone breathes that hard oughtn't to be carryin' a knife. Strain their heart."

"You think so, do you?" Vin shouted, coming up from the ground. Doggone it, he had come as close to apologizing as anyone could expect for such a thing. "Let's try fists, then!"

Everyone stayed in position as if stunnned. Mark frowned, bit back words Vin knew were a rebuke. Jare winced. And Roncador's breath rumbled uneasily in his mashed nose. Evidently they all were granting Vin the privilege to make a fool of himself, that freedom of grownups.

Clance very calmly surveyed him for a second; then he leaned back against the wagon, folding his arms. "Listen a minute and then if you still want it, I'll bust your nose for you. I've been told you got a burr under the saddle and what it is, and I can sure savvy how you want to fight. But do you think Rip Ford needs sulky kids? Tarnation, boy! You think I'm here because I want it?" Clance straightened indignantly. "I'm one of Ford's old Rangers but he wouldn't let me join this last shenanigan after I came all the way from El Paso in a wagon! He said, 'Clance, you got an old bullet in your thigh and you can't sit your saddle like you'd have to.' Wouldn't listen to anything I said. Told me moving this cotton was important. And then *you*," Clance pointed a scrawny finger, "you act like you were the onliest one with troubles!"

Stripped to the bone, Vin could only flush, stare at the ground. It was hard, grinding hard, but he forced his gaze to meet Clance's, gulped, and found a rusty voice.

"I'm sorry. I—I guess I wouldn't be much of a soldier yet."

Clance thrust out his hand. "You'll make one," he said, twinkling. "Temper's a good thing. Got to keep a lid on it, though, like gunpowder."

Vin sat up. He sang *Dixie* as loud as anyone till Jare got tired of playing and they all went to bed.

If the drive to the border last summer and fall was bad, the present journey was wretched. The wind that had scorched then, now jabbed freezing, cunning gusts down collars, up sleeves and pants' legs, through blankets and coats. They still ate swirling dust, but in spite of the cold, there was miserably little rain, and they made more dry camps than not. Their animals would have perished if they hadn't gotten some moisture from the broad cactus leaves. More than once the men chewed these, too, saving their canteens for morning coffee or dire need.

"Well," grunted Vin one night, breath steaming pale in the dim light, "there shouldn't be many bandits out. If I were one, I'd hole up in this kind of weather!"

"*Ay*," grinned Diego, making one of his rare comments, "they don't have to stay out in it. One gang, which the Gray Ghost hanged last month, had a shelter built into the side of a ravine. Out of this awful wind, *señores*, snug as what you call it—a flea in a rug? They would stay there *muy contento*, playing cards, drinking *tequila*, till their lookouts saw travelers. Whish! A few hours' work, maybe, and back to their leisure."

He sounded so wistful the others laughed.

"But Benavides hung them," Mark reminded.

"Yes," agreed Diego, brightening. "That is true. They were not lucky after all."

One night when Jare's hands were too raw for fiddling,

Clance, at Vin's questioning, talked of Ford and the Ranger days.

"It was about four-and-a-half years when Cortina, the border bandit, took over Brownsville and whipped all the militia that attacked him. The border was like a battlefield, people afraid to stir out of their homes. The governor of Texas met Rip on an Austin street and says, 'Colonel Ford, you've got to take an army down there and straighten things out.' "

Even Jare's eyes glowed with interest, and Vin leaned forward. "What happened?"

"We rode down Congress street and ferried the Colorado. Then we took that trip to the Rio."

"How many were in the army?" Vin pressed, seeing in his mind hundreds of hard-bitten carbine-carrying Rangers riding fast and gallant on prancing horses to put down the outlaw.

"Well," drawled Clance, poker-faced, "there were eight of us."

"Eight!"

Clance nodded. "Yep, With a few guns, a little grub—and not a red cent of public money. The Texas State Treasury was broke."

"How did you make out?" queried Mark with raised eyebrows.

"Oh, at Goliad we got some money, and later some supplies. By the time we hit the border we had over fifty armed men. That many Rangers under Ford *is* an army. We chased Cortina up and down till he vanished in the hills back of Guerrero. He didn't come back, either, till this war started and he saw a fine chance to make trouble."

"Hates gringos," mused Warren, shifting tobacco. "Claims they stole his family's land."

"May have," admitted Clance, "but he's got four or five

ranches in Mexico now, and he stocks 'em with stolen Texas cattle."

During the long noonings, Clance and Roncador usually gave Vin a workout with the knife. From his hunting he had a trained, quick eye and was soon pleasing his teachers. To protect themselves, they wrapped a coat or blanket around the left forearm. Clance explained it was also possible to entangle an enemy's knife in the cloth and hold it while striking home.

"Meanest knife-man I ever knew, Natchez river pilot, used his bare arm to take the other feller's blade," Clance said. "Caught the steel 'tween his bones, he did. Then he'd give his arm a twist so's to hold the knife, and he'd drive his into the other man."

Jare, looking sick, turned away. With a shiver, Vin said, "That took nerve!"

"Yep. But he got his man. Had nasty scars all over his left forearm."

Roncador snorted. "I'm not taking any knife less'n it's forced on me!"

Which was how Vin felt. But he hunted the place on his arm, between the bones, where a knife could fit. The idea made him queasy. He called to Jare, "Strings on the fiddle broken or something?" and felt better when the dark boy started playing. Funny. When things were hardest, they all counted on the music. And when Jare played *Dixie,* it made them feel they were part of the Confederacy, that they were, down in this obscure gritty desert, taking a stand for it.

It was during a noon halt when a horseman came in sight. He was alone, but all the men except Jare got in reach of their weapons, and resumed their eating. Squinting up from gravy and biscuits, Vin caught something familiar about the swing of the body, the proud set of neck and head.

Paco!

Vin kept seated with an effort. Wild conjectures leaped through his head. Had Paco, learning he hadn't gone to Missouri, come to settle his grudge right now? If he had, Vin could at least hold a knife right. But Paco, coming to the ground, with a tremor of the legs that showed he had ridden a long time, ignored him and greeted Mark.

"My commander has assigned me to ride scout for you. He is presently escorting a large train several days south, so more men could not be spared."

Doggoned if we don't always get you, though, Vin thought.

"Thanks," Mark nodded. "Unsaddle and eat. Glad to have you."

Paco tended his horse, filled a plate, and hunkered down by Jare. He cast a glance of bright malice at Vin. "So you are still with the wagons instead of an army?"

"You spend a fair amount of time with the wagons yourself," Vin gave back. Paco scowled.

"Can I help it if we get a messenger from the Captain King saying you have left San Antonio shorthanded, and a scout, at the least, is needed?" Paco brooded. "I had thought he would run out of cotton, but no, some girl who refuged at the ranch after Brownsville had marked down the location of several cotton caches she saw, and I hear she is a partner with Captain King in this!"

Vin spluttered. So that was Estrella's "business"! She wouldn't be around Mother long before her cash went to supply hospital demands, if she hadn't already used it for the Vargas kids. He swallowed his dislike of Paco to ask, "Do you know if this girl has been heard from since she left the ranch?"

"She has left?" Paco shrugged philosophically. "I was hoping to meet a lady both enterprising, and from what I've heard, *muy linda*. That is life."

"She doesn't like soldiers," Vin snubbed.

"Then she must be your sweetheart," gibed Paco.

Jare, making peace in sober, earnest fashion, declared, "I'd be honored if Miss Estrella thought of me as a friend."

This was so like Jare that Vin had to laugh and couldn't be mad enough to roll Paco in the dust as he had been about to do. He said with reasonable good nature, "I reckon we won't discuss ladies."

Paco inclined his curly head. But later as they were breaking camp, he came up to Vin, pointed at his knife.

"You can use that Bowie?"

"Some."

"Study it," Paco advised. "Become dexterous."

"Why?"

"Plainly, so that we may have a worthy battle at the proper time." White teeth showed in careless pleasure. "I will even teach you some of my good tricks."

"Thanks, no," Vin said. He gave the other boy a look of wonderment. "I think even if you had a bullet in your head you'd still be thinking on this silly duel!"

"How can you call it silly? Fate conspires to bring us together." The slender boy's grin changed to a pained frown. *"Caramba!* But I did not think to have to go long miles with you again, watch your ears flap like one of your mules!"

"Keep on," warned Vin, "and we'll do some more of that cheap, gringo wrestlin' you don't like."

Paco drifted with a derisive crow. He swung into his saddle and made a show of curveting while Vin climbed to the wagon seat and hollered at the mules.

THE CONFEDERATE FIDDLE

Vin intended to fist-fight Paco if he kept crowding, and the arrogant young soldier seemed to sense this, for he left off his heckling. To Vin's surprise, he made himself useful at the halts, helping with Roncador's team so the cook could get meals, and also joining in the forage for cactus leaves. He had a pleasant deep voice, and Spanish songs filled their evenings now as often as Missouri music. Almost miraculously, they met no bandits.

"I think perhaps this new smuggler, 'El Brazo,' has scared off the little outlaws," Paco mused one evening when the subject came up. "It is strange. He does not bother the wagons so long as they are in Texas, though his band has been sighted riding at a distance from occasional trains. Once the loads are transferred to foreign merchants, though, for the trip to Mata-moros, this El Brazo attacks. He has been very successful."

The Arm. "That's an odd name," Vin said. "What does he look like?"

"No one knows. He wears a mask. I do not know why he does that since his having only one arm identifies him any-way."

It seemed there were some paths to wealth open to one-armed men after all; but Vin was glad Darcy wouldn't be taking this one. "Why doesn't Colonel Benavides catch him?"

Paco shrugged. "El Brazo does his actual robbery in Mex-

ico. Cheno Cortina is after him. Let the Mexicans handle it."
Clance chortled.

"Somebody beating Cheno at his own game! I'll bet he
doesn't like it! Even if he is a bandit I kind of like the sound
of this El Brazo."

The back of Vin's neck prickled. "That's dandy for you,"
he said, "but remember, I still have to get to Matamoros down
the Mexican side of the river." Paco eyed him mournfully.

"That is a pity. Maybe we don't get our duel."

Jare spoke thoughtfully, "If there's no big press on me to
bring a wagon back from Laredo, perhaps I could go along
with thee, Vin. Getting that violin sold and all your money
exchanged for drugs is as important as anything else I could
help with."

"But you won't fight," Vin argued.

"There might be something else I could do."

"What?" In spite of himself, sarcasm crept into Vin's tone.
"I don't think El Brazo will let us by for your playing him a
pretty tune."

Back stiffening like a ramrod, Paco erupted. "You insult
my friend who tries to aid you? Churl! Well, I shall beg my
commander to let me go with you, too. I *can* fight. And now
it is necessary to my honor to preserve your hide that I may
carve it later!"

"Hah!" snorted Vin. "You talk a bloody battle but it's always in the future! And Jare was my friend before he laid
eyes on you!"

"You are a fine friend, to jeer at his music!"

Both boys were on their feet, glaring. Jare got between
them. "Friends," he pleaded, *"Amigos!* If thee truly have liking for me, don't fight. Shall we try, then, to journey from
Laredo together?"

Vin looked at Paco. He said grudgingly, "If you can stay civil, come if you want. The Strad needs all the protection it can get."

"I can treat you like a thin-shelled egg," smiled Paco. "For I shall be thinking of—the future."

Mark said drily, "I feel for the wagon train you three join. Don't let 'em tear you apart, Jare." Jare bowed a trill from the Confederate fiddle.

"Oh, we'll get along," he said.

How the Quaker boy would be anything but a drag in a fight was beyond Vin, but he did appreciate Jare's offer and was sorry for his rudeness. He told Jare, "I am glad you're coming. And—and I know it's braver of you not to fight than to do it. I don't understand you but I do finally understand that."

Paco nodded. "That," he grinned, "is how it is with me, also. And that is the first intelligent thing I've ever heard you say."

Vin stiffened, but when everyone laughed, he did, too, and retorted, "Thousand thanks. You're sounding more like a human being yourself!" Then they ignored each other and listened to Jare play.

It was late in February when they came to Laredo. King's agents disposed of the cotton to speculators who would now move it down to sell in Matamoros. Benavides granted Paco's request to accompany Jare and Vin with the Stradivarius, for El Brazo still ranged the border, challenging Cortina for its lordship. It was known that the red-bearded Mexican was after the new bandit in earnest, not only from personal jealousy but also because his government was losing much revenue from the bales El Brazo seized.

And Rip Ford?

To his anxious questions, Vin got a discouraging but not hopeless answer. Ford and his recruits had left San Antonio and were headed for the King Ranch, keeping in touch constantly with the border forces under Benavides. Probably, when the Union position had been properly spied out and Ford had laid his plans, he would join with Benavides and try to dislodge the immensely larger Union army from its grip on the lower Rio Grande and the strategic route to Matamoros. Right now there were many Union irregulars and plain thieves deviling the King Ranch. Ford must want first to drub them out of the vicinity of that great cotton depot before attending to the Rio.

A Union base at Corpus Christi could have completely knocked out the ranch as a cotton center, and that was what the Union commander at Fort Brown kept urging. Fortunately, his superiors stayed as blind to border strategy as Davis' Confederate cabinet. The cotton continued to roll through Laredo and Eagle Pass while the Yanks at Fort Brown made useless sorties upriver, cursing the brush into which Benavides vanished like the ghost he was called.

"Maybe you can trade off that fiddle and get with old Rip after all," said Clance wistfully. "Or maybe he'll take Fort Brown whilst you're in Matamoros, and you can just cross over and join up. You just remember what I've showed you with that Bowie."

Paco smiled. "He'd better remember!"

Jare looked miserable and Mark cut through their talk to say to the Quaker boy, "We'll miss that fiddle. It's helped through many a nasty night. Seems a shame for the Confederacy to lose it."

"Well," Jare pointed out, "they'll be getting it back in the form of medicine." He added shyly, "I'm glad it's not going to buy guns."

Vin, considering it for the first time, was surprised to find he agreed. Why? He couldn't say. It was just that it would have seemed sad to change the music of the violin for instruments of death. Since it had to be sold, he was glad it would buy solace for hurt and dying men.

In exchange for their help as drivers, the three boys got places with a cotton train, and permission to stow the blanketed fiddle in a wagon. Mark, Roncador, and the other teamsters would be taking back war supplies to be sent northeast. They all had one last camp night together, in the comparative comfort of a stable, and the Confederate fiddle sang as if it knew it would soon be in alien hands.

Annie Laurie, Juanita, Listen to the Mockingbird—these, and many others, all the songs they could remember, with Mark's rollicking tenor vibrating over the less assured voices. *Dixie* came last. Vin went to sleep with it echoing in his mind and heart. If he could just get to Ford in time to help drive out the Yankees, he wouldn't, in the long run, regret this last drive to the border.

He had learned a lot on it. To handle his temper better in spite of disappointments; the use of the Bowie; how to get the best from a thirsty, fagged team; more understanding of different kinds of men from being with Clance and Warren, Diego and Raul. Also, though he couldn't keep the fiddle for the family, he could give them stories of it that would bear proud telling for generations.

Next morning he said good-bye to Mark, Roncador and the

other teamsters. With Jare and Paco, the cotton money in his belt, he crossed into the Mexican Laredo and searched out their wagon train and its captain, a blond German immigrant from the San Antonio region. A lot of these men, newly come to the United States and feeling the war had nothing to do with them, had taken jobs that exempted them from conscription, though others had hurried to enlist as if to prove their new allegiance. Vin could see it would be puzzling. They had come, after all, to the United States, not the Confederacy.

Reich, the wagonmaster, greeted them heartily and asked to examine the violin. His northern blue eyes shone as his calloused fingers caressed the wood.

"*Ach,* maybe now it goes back to where it came from," he murmured. "But it must be sad for you, young sir, to lose this beautiful thing. We will see it is not crowded and yet fits snugly enough not to bang around."

He personally oversaw this and then assigned the boys to wagons. Vin and Jare were teamed together while Paco took an empty place on a different wagon. The drivers were bringing up their teams, hitching them to their loads. As Vin and Jare harnessed the animals Reich indicated as theirs, Vin saw a vaguely familiar figure some distance away busying himself with adjusting a wagon seat. The voice in which he called commands to an unseen helper on the other side rang hauntingly in Vin's ear. The man straightened, black tie swinging free from a dirty ruffled white shirt front, and Vin gasped.

"I'll be dogged! Wardell Beauregard Jims! And Sancho!" For the invisible assistant had moved around, revealing himself to be the pudgy follower of the pretended cotton agent who had months ago given Vin his welcome to Texas.

"That's not all," Jare exclaimed. "Look yonder—the man who can't get his harness straight. Trig Medders!"

Vin almost staggered. "All the rascals in a clutch," he breathed. "I'm going to tell Captain Reich what he's got here!"

But Reich spread big helpless palms. "I believe what you say of these men, but whom am I to hire? Most teamsters who come from the United States to work in Mexico are desperate men, but I must move my wagons. Ignore them and I am sure they will leave you alone."

"They're traitors and thieves!" Vin protested.

"I am sorry," said Reich, tone chilling. "You may wait for another train if you wish. But if you travel with mine, you must not start trouble. All I am concerned with is fulfilling my contract."

Vin knew no other train was being formed and it would be at least a week and probably longer before one was ready. A precious week, which might mean the difference between his joining Ford or missing him.

"All right," he shrugged. "You're the captain."

As he went back to his team, Trig called to him, "Howdy, Clayburn! Tattle-taling already? It won't do you any good down here, boy." And then, on a note of rising glee, "Durned if the cute little feller ain't got him a knife! Is it a play-purty or for real?"

"Mind your own business or you may find out," Vin said.

Jims, who had been listening, coughed genteelly and said in his rolling voice, "Now, lads, it behooves us as comrades to bury old grudges and put our shoulders to the wheel of our common venture. Let bygones go by, that's the spirit."

"I haven't lost my mind—or my memory," returned Vin. "Leave us alone and we'll do you the same favor."

"Huh!" whistled Trig. "To have a Quaker boy for a running-mate, he sure talks mean!" Sancho leered, but Jims spoke sorrowfully.

"Leave him in his stiff-neckedness, Trig. Let us not have it said we fanned the cankering flames of vendetta."

Vin, climbing into the wagon, said to Jare, "That old hypocrite! I'm going to sleep with one eye open, that's for sure!"

"They're not reliable," Jare said in such a gravely regretful tone that Vin had to laugh. Reich gave the starting signal and the wagons lumbered into order. Though it was two hundred miles to Matamoros, this was the last leg of the long trip and Vin looked at his mules' ears with something like affection as he yelled and flicked them and tightened the reins.

This crew, made up as it was of strays and men of different nationalities, broke up in little groups for meals and leisure. Vin, Paco, and Jare kept to themselves, but when Jare played the Strad of nights the other men slowly drifted close. Reich especially loved the music. Several times he walked off hastily, blowing his nose. He told Jare the playing reminded him of home and the wonderful music he had heard in Berlin and Heidelberg. Even Jims haunched his gaunt frame into a dreamy pose to listen, but Sancho and Trig lay over by their fire and raced fleas or played dice.

Winter was giving way to a cruel spring, the drouth merely a warm one now instead of freezing. At least, though, they could water their beasts in the Rio. The road, full of chugholes and bumps, was unbelievably bad, even after the routes Vin had experienced. It didn't seem to matter. Each creaking mile, each hour took him nearer. Once the Strad was sold, nothing could possibly come up to interfere with his getting into the fight. He even began to forget about El Brazo. Per-

haps Cortina had caught his rival. The train was half-way to
Matamoros, and their only difficulties had been natural ones,
with the wagons, roads, and mules.

Of course Vin had his own personal difficulties, with Trig.
At first, sensing Reich's liking for the Missouri boys, Trig had
left them alone, except for an occasional jeer. But as the days
wore on and the monotony began to fray tempers, Trig began
to pick at Jare. He knew Jare wouldn't retaliate, and he also
knew better than to do his teasing when the fiery Paco might
hear. Vin, raised in the frontier code of letting each person
stand on his own feet, didn't feel he should mix in unless Trig
did Jare bodily harm. If a person didn't believe in defending
himself he could scarcely expect anyone else to. But Paco's
loyalties were ferociously simple. He would have taken on
Trig for the fun of it.

The strange thing was that Jare apparently minded less
than Vin. As Trig addressed his raw, heckling taunts to the
Quaker boy, Jare seemed not to hear, but Vin, seething, would
feel himself turning red and start to breathe fast.

"Why don't you poke him?" he demanded furiously.

Jare shook his head. "What would that solve?"

"It'd solve his saying these things to you!"

Jare said what he had evidently worked out in his mind.
"What he says is a poison working out of him like pus from
a sore. Perhaps if it comes out, the poison will drain and leave
him well. If he can't get rid of it, it will finally kill him."

"He's a permanent case of gangrene," Vin snorted.

But Jare would not argue. "You're just as provoking as
Trig," Vin accused in helpless wrath. "You've got nobody to
blame but yourself that he plagues you!"

"Was I blaming thee?"

Vin gulped, choked, and yelled at the mules. When he could

trust his voice again, he said, "Mules aren't stubborn. They're really not—at least not after a person knows you, Jare Wheelright!"

Jare laughed. After a minute, so did Vin. He could never understand Jare, and he really didn't want to because it made him uncomfortable about his own ideas. But he liked him; yes, he did. And—well, something was going to be done about Trig.

It was April now and the days were growing hot. After supper, Vin itched so with grime and heat that he faded away from Jare's music and went to the river. Slow-moving and dirty, it was a far cry from the clear, limestone-bottomed Missouri creeks, but at least it was *wet*. Draping his clothes over a scrub willow, Vin waded in, swam lazily up and down the brownish current, as night set in.

Those leather patches Estrella had put on his clothes were pulling the worn cloth around them till he'd be lucky to reach Matamoros in any state of modesty. Where were Mother, Estrella, Aunt Rachel and Uncle Jess? Could they have gotten to Richmond? It worried him to think about them, besides giving him a funny, lonesome feeling in the pit of his stomach, so he shifted his thoughts. They immediately fixed on Darcy.

Where could he have gone? Hired out on a blockade-runner? Vin couldn't imagine Darcy, quick-silver, excitement-loving Darcy, working in a store or office. Besides, these weren't places to make money fast and that was what Darcy had said he would do. The best place to get rich was speculating in cotton and war supplies but that would take some money to begin with. Vin sighed, escaping from the river and his troubling questions.

He just hoped Darcy wouldn't turn wild, go sour, bitter. Darcy needed his arm. Yes, more than most men, he needed it, for he wasn't used to getting along without what he wanted. And he had been so deft and skilful with his hands—for one of them to be wasted, it wasn't fair! Not be a surgeon; not to play the violin; not to have both arms to hold a girl. How would Darcy live with the things naturally intended for him denied him for good? Vin couldn't stand the idea and walked fast, almost running, towards the campfires.

Why wasn't Jare playing?

Through the silence rose angry voices. Among the firelit silhouettes, two had come to their feet. Vin got to the circle as Paco challenged, blade glittering in his hand, "Come now, gringo! Is your tongue your only weapon?"

Jare, laying aside the violin, caught his friend's sleeve. "Please, Paco! His words don't hurt me." Evidently Trig had forgotten his caution and gibed at Jare in front of Paco who shook free of the Quaker boy.

"My Jare, you are too good and this fool does not understand that! But he will understand me!"

Trig had gone pasty-white even in the glow of the ruddy fire. He stared at the knife and licked his lips. "I—I cain't handle a frogsticker near as well as you," he whined. "It's not your fight anyhow. You got no business jumpin' me."

Paco laughed.

"Cap'n!" yelled Trig, glancing around in terror. "Cap'n, you won't let this Meskin carve me up, will you?"

"I have been tired of your big mouth for some time," observed Reich. "You need teaching. And if the lesson kills you it won't be much loss."

Paco came of knife people. He was expert and icy-furious.

Trig would be lucky to come out alive. Maybe he did deserve it but Vin couldn't watch. He tapped Paco on the arm.

"Let me take him."

"He is mine!"

"He is afraid, Paco. You'd find no honor in it."

Chewing his lip a minute, Paco finally nodded. "Well, then." He added more cheerfully, "At least it will give you more practice towards our appointment."

Trig, who had been carrying a knife to dances since Vin was twelve years old and was hence sure of his superiority with the weapon, grinned with relief and strutted forward. "Get out your purty knife, Clayburn. I'm ready!"

He lunged as Vin drew his Bowie, sidestepped to narrowly avoid Trig's blade. The treacherous attack turned Vin white-hot angry. Trig had an Arkansas toothpick. Thrust, parry, feint, guard. Vin's body remembered its training. Fire on the blades, heavy breathing and calls from the watchers. Dust kicked up from Trig's shifting feet.

Sweat dripped from Vin, his heart drummed, his breath grew into a throttling pain. He caught Trig's knife on his thumbguard, heard it slip across the soft metal. Trig moved in closer.

His yellow eyes had dilated with pupil till they were almost black. He panted, teeth peeled back from his lips. In his eyes showed the start of fear; he wasn't fighting a complete novice. But perhaps because he had acted the coward with Paco, perhaps because he could not bear to retreat from a younger boy he had known always and patronized, Trig frantically pressed Vin, slashing, leaving himself open. Parrying and ducking, Vin could have sent his Bowie several times into Trig's body, yet he somehow didn't. He didn't want to kill, he learned now when he had the chance and every provocation. And even if he had wanted to, with Jare watching it would have been impossible.

Yet Vin was getting desperate. He was exhausted, couldn't keep up this defensive fighting forever. He had to stop Trig. But how, without driving home the Bowie? Then Vin remembered Clance's story—the riverman who used his arm to catch knives while he killed.

When Trig's blade flashed in next time, Vin set his teeth, took the knife in his arm. It grated on a bone. Sweating, praying, he forced his arm under and held the blade.

EL BRAZO

Through the searing red pain, Vin heard indrawn breaths and a flutter of cries. "Get 'im, youngster!" "Now you've got the big blowhard!" And from Paco came an admiring call on all his saints. Sick through from the grate of steel on his bones, Vin looked at Trig through dancing hazes of red and black, so maddened with pain and the thirsty, urging voices around him that he raised the Bowie. But he saw the mute dread in Trig's eyes, the pleading for life from another human being.

Vin sheathed his knife, freed his arm, stumbled away. "I don't need to kill you," he said.

Amid unbelieving murmurs of protest and wonder, Vin gratefully let Jare help him sit down by a wagon. Reich brought a flask of *mescal,* dumped the burning liquid over the wound. As he bandaged Vin's arm, checking the bones, Reich muttered in German, translating at length for their benefit, "I have seen many duels, even fought them. But a thing like this I have never seen. Brave—and crazy!"

Paco hunkered down by Vin. He said awkwardly, "I do not want that duel now, *amigo.* You are too much for me, I think!" Vin laughed.

"I'm glad to hear it. This was enough dueling to last me the rest of my life!"

Jare didn't say anything, but the shine in his eyes made

Vin feel good—clean and spacious and ten feet tall. Into this circle of well-being, a smooth sonorous voice uncoiled.

"My admiration for the young hero cannot dull appreciation of the ideal moment for action. Gentlemen, those of you with weapons, do not attempt to use them. Those without, do not attempt to reach one. You are under three guns—and though young Trig may not fight well against armed men, I assure you he is formidable against helpless ones!"

Swinging around, the surprised teamsters stared into guns held by Jims, Sancho, and Trig, each at an angle from each other so that they covered the group. Reich's hand streaked for his pistol. Before it came free of the holster, Jims' gun barked and blood welled from Reich's shoulder.

"Can't blame you for trying, Captain," Jims said pleasantly. "But our next shots kill. You're warned."

"You're not El Brazo?" Reich choked.

"Only his helper. I pointed out to him how much simpler it would be to take a train from inside, as it were. The notion appealed to him. He is a humane lad and would rather not have murder. Trig, you build our signal fire now. He was expecting it during the third week from Laredo and that is this one, so he'll be near. Oh, but first, my boy, collect the weapons from these gentlemen. We don't want anyone to get hurt, do we?" And he beamed graciously at the astounded camp.

Jare moved towards Captain Reich. Trig threatened, but Jims said benevolently, "By all means bind up the Captain's arm, son. Douse some of that *mescal* on it and give me the rest of the bottle."

Trig yanked away Vin's Bowie, jostling his sore arm.

"You," said Vin, "sure are a snake."

Trig pushed his face up to Vin's. "And you're a highfalutin' Clayburn, huh? Well, let me tell you, boy, you're in for a shock!" He passed on with a nasty grin.

"You should have killed him!" rasped Paco, staring regretfully after his confiscated knife. "What did he mean?"

"Can't even guess," Vin shrugged. He helped Jare with the Captain's arm. Then, under the guns of the three bandits, the teamsters sat down to wait for El Brazo.

"We are all rather nervous," Jims said after a while. "Why do you not play the violin, young Jare? It will perhaps ease the wounds of your friends, and make our trigger fingers less jumpy."

"Shall I?" Jare asked Vin.

Vin raised a shoulder, let it fall. "It'd be better than just sitting here watching those three buzzards."

First Jare played a German tune Captain Reich had taught him, then some hill songs, and *vaquero* music. But when he played *Bonnie Blue Flag,* Trig's face darkened and as *Dixie* began, Jims stirred and said harshly, "Another tune, if you please!"

But Jare played on as if he hadn't heard.

"Blast you!" snarled Trig, leveling his gun.

Vin sprang to knock Jare to safety in the same instant that Trig fired and a voice cried from the darkness, "What is this? What's the music—?"

Still kneeling, Vin froze. That voice. He knew it, like a part of himself that had been lost. And while his mind groped after what his heart already grasped, ten men rode into the camp. The leader, on a ghost-gray horse, wore a cape and soft, broad hat that hid the side of his face. He reined his horse with his left hand. Then the cape blew free and Vin saw the empty right sleeve.

El Brazo. Only . . .

"Darcy!" Vin cried. "Darcy!" And because he could not believe it but because it was true, he called his brother's name again as if it would break to bits on his tongue. "Oh, Darcy—"

The cloaked figure stiffened. Slowly, the face turned. Vin looked up at his brother, at the empty sleeve, at the trappings of a border bandit, and felt sick, strange, and light, as if his heart were breaking while his brain worked on.

Darcy's eyes burned from dark hollows to peer at Vin, and the high cheekbones stood out above the gashed flatness running into the lean jaw Vin remembered. But the face was like a mask of Darcy's, set in lines Vin had never seen. Then these lines cracked and that was somehow worse.

Darcy turned on Trig. "You signaled me down on my own brother."

A buzz ran through the teamsters and bandits as they understood. Trig said blusteringly, "I signaled you down on a train. What difference does it make who's on it?"

"For you," said Darcy with a hard little laugh, "about the difference in breathing and not. You've got three seconds to shoot or run."

"You high-mighty Clayburns!" Trig exploded. Rage and fear lit off a desperate courage in him; perhaps he thought Darcy's left hand was slow enough to beat. He raised his pistol. Darcy's left hand flashed. He fired from his hip, on the draw.

Trig crumpled, his charge harmlessly eroding the dust as he fell to it. El Brazo—Vin could not think of him as Darcy now—commanded his men.

"Guard the teamsters but do not shoot unless necessary. Jims, get a grave dug for that carrion." Tossing his reins to one of his followers, El Brazo swung to the ground. He looked from Vin to Jare, stared at the fiddle.

"Is—that the Strad?"

Vin nodded. He felt as if his heart and throat were weeping blood inside, strangling him. Oh, Darcy, Darcy—*you!* He couldn't look at his brother who had committed murder as if just to prove who he was. Trembling, nauseated till he wished he could fall to his knees, Vin felt his brother's hand on him and flinched.

"Straighten up!" Darcy snapped. Vin saw shame and fury and confusion in his brother's eyes. "I—I'd give anything for this not to have happened, but it has and you can't fold up like a girl. What're you doing this side of the river? Where'd you get the Strad?"

Iron suddenly entered Vin. He gave Darcy's gaze back and stood every bit as tall. "Our mother brought it. All the way to the King Ranch. And the heirloom furniture and the silver." Darcy went pale.

"Things are that bad at home?"

"You never went home to see, did you?" Vin demanded, blood pounding wildly in his ears. "You had to get a lot of money to take the place of your arm. Well, Pa's dead, killed by guerillas, And Mother's gone to work at the hospital in Richmond where she went to hunt for you." *How will she stand it—what you've done?*

It was between them like a shout, louder than if it'd been spoken. Darcy stood numbly a moment. Then he walked over and leaned against a wagon. When he spoke, he had control of his voice but it had a lash-edge of madness.

"Pa—dead? And Mother in that rotten place? Why—why did she go there?"

"Because she wanted to help." Vin saw his words were stabbing Darcy like knives, but he couldn't blunt them. "That's why she had me sell the things, why I'm taking this fiddle to Matamoros. The money is to buy drugs, medicines."

Darcy glanced involuntarily at his empty sleeve. Remembering the operation without sedatives, thinking of what his mother would be watching daily? Realizing the difference between what he was and the surgeon he had intended to be? Darcy folded his cape around his shoulder, hiding his lack of an arm. He gave Vin an appraising stare as if, for the first time, he saw a person, not a kid brother.

"And I guess this errand is what has kept you out of the army?"

"I'm joining Rip Ford's command as quick as I get the medicines bought and on their way—if I do," Vin corrected. He looked around at the circle of outlaws, at Jims and Sancho who were beginning to fidget. Darcy saw, too, from the corner of his eye.

Deliberately, he kept his back turned. "I could save the Strad for you, Vin. But the rest of this cargo is already gold in their pockets to my men. They won't let it go."

So this was the way it was going to have to be.

Vin wavered. At least he could salvage the fidddle. Reich was in this game for profit, anyway, and had known his risks. No one would be hurt. With the cotton, El Brazo and his men would ride away—

No. Because El Brazo *was* Darcy, Darcy, his brother, and it was on his conscience, what Darcy did. Vin shook his head.

"I'll have to fight you, Darcy."

Darcy's eyes flashed. He bulked tall in the night a minute; then with a sigh, he appeared to relax. He said, smiling, "No, kid, you won't fight me. *We'll* fight them. I'll slip you my other gun—it's loaded—under my cape, and you hide it in your shirt. I'm going to promote a little party. While it's on, you alert all the teamsters you can to be ready for my play. Tell 'em to have a man singled out and dive for him when I tip our hand." As Darcy faced about, Vin felt cold metal in his hand, eased it into his shirt where it was out of sight because of the leather vest that hung free, concealing the bulge.

Raising his arm, Darcy, laughing, called in his men. "I have found my little brother, *amigos!*" he shouted. "Juan, Candelario, you stand guard first while we have a celebration!"

"Celebration?" muttered Sancho. "Why do we need a celebration?"

"Because my brother joins me—and he is *muy valiente,* a good man to have. Jims, you'll know where all the *mescal* and *tequila* is stashed. Break it out!" Darcy put his arm around Jare, pulling him towards the light. "Here we have a fine musician. Everything for a *fandango* except the girls!"

Catching the spirit, several of the bandits began to whoop, darting from wagon to wagon and exhuming the private jugs of certain teamsters. One clapped Vin on the back.

"El Brazo's brother! Hola! How will the border survive?"

Jare had started playing, rowdy swinging tunes to spread the fever. Vin came up behind Paco who gave him a cold stare. "So! Had you planned this with your brother all the time?"

"Shut up and listen!" Vin hissed. "The party's a fake. When it's going good, Darcy's going to make a play. Pick a man and go for him when you see it's time."

When this sunk in, Paco's eyes flamed. *"Bueno!"* He estimated the distance to the heap of weapons beside Jims. "I can get my knife, I think, before that beanpole can shoot!"

"Pass the word on to anyone you trust," Vin whispered and moved on before he was noticed.

In this fashion, while the bandits were occupied with drink and music and roaring at Darcy's jokes, Vin eased among the teamsters, warning those he thought would prove handy in the fight. He felt the gun Darcy had slipped him tug heavily at his clothing. His vision was unusually sharp and it seemed he could hear the breathing of all the men, feel their blood pounding along with his.

Only Jims and Sancho had not entered into the party. They sat frowning and puzzled, perhaps because they knew Vin and doubted his sudden switch to outlawry. Jims at last got up and came over to Darcy. Vin drifted into earshot.

Now, his tense nerves screamed. *Now . . .*

"Brazo," said Jims, "I can sympathize with your joy at recruiting your brother—an extraordinary lad. But this is hardly the time to relax. May I suggest we make off with the wagons and rollick later?"

Darcy said absently, "In a moment, Jims, in a moment. I want to see if I can play this thing." And he took the Stradivarius from Jare. Leaning it against his right shoulder, he huddled over it, trying to use the bow, but got only discords, wailings. For a second, his face contorted, his eyes closed. Then he was the leader again, erect, smiling, as he turned to Vin.

"Well, kid, I guess I can't play any more. So—" He smashed the fiddle across Jims' head, felling him, grabbed his gun, and got Sancho who had fired the same instant.

The circle erupted into a madhouse. Paco's knife was out. Other teamsters grabbed their unguarded weapons. In a few shrieking moments the bandits were dead or running.

Vin dropped on his knees by Darcy. Darcy tried to sit, failed, and gasped, "Sorry I—broke the Strad, Vin. In my belt—lots of gold. Get drugs with it." He fell back, his hand trailing across the broken strings of the fiddle.

Vin sat in the dust and held his brother.

They buried Darcy with the Stradivarius, his arm clasped around it. "He died well," Paco said. "I think—I think the rest should be forgotten."

Reich nodded. "Yes, and though it will leave me short-handed, I'd like you boys to take some of the dead bandits' horses and go ahead to Matamoros for those medicines. I still have my cargo—which I wouldn't have without your help."

Six weeks later in the May sunshine, packs and saddlebags heavy with precious medicines, the three boys paused on the banks of Mexico, looking across at Fort Ringgold where Ford had rendezvoused with Benavides and set up headquarters. Paco had this knowledge from a friend they had met in Reynosa two days ago. Vin wouldn't have far to go now to join Rip Ford.

Jare said, "I left Darcy's fiddle with Mark. Shall I send it to you?" For Jare was rejoining the wagons and would personally see their load of drugs as far as possible on its journey to Richmond.

A letter would have to go along, telling something about Darcy's death, but not all. Mother would feel better to know that though Darcy was buried in Mexico, he had the Confederate fiddle with him; he had inherited it after all, though he could not play it. Darcy could not have lived long without music anyway; to have become El Brazo had been the start of dying. But at the end he had taken on himself his responsibility. That was what Vin would remember, what he would tell.

Now, to Jare's question, he shook his head. "No, you keep the fiddle." He thought of Estrella and Mother, wondered when they would all get back to Missouri, what it would be like, what they would do. "After the war, we'll be going home. Whichever side wins, Jare, we'll need music—and people like you." For though Jare's way of peace could not be his, Vin valued it and saw in it the hope for a time of no wars. Paco stretched tall in his stirrups.

"*Ay!*" he said, laughing to the morning, "there'll always be music. But how about breakfast?"

The boys nudged their horses and splashed into the river.